Best Man for the Job

Book One of:
The Men of Fear Incorporated Series

By Melinda Valentine

Best Man for the Job

Limitless Publishing, LLC
Kailua, HI 96734
www.limitlesspublishing.com

Formatting: Limitless Publishing

ISBN-13: 978-1-68058-675-6
ISBN-10: 1-68058-675-0

Mike,
Thanks for Reading
Much Love.
~Melinda Valentine

Dedication

For my family.
For your encouragement.
For your faith.
For your love.
This is for you.

Chapter One

Max

Maxwell entered the club, brushing past a large, brutish-looking bouncer. The room was poorly lit, no doubt to hide the stains and tears in the carpet and upholstery. It smelled of smoke, sweat, and arousal. Why he'd agreed to come here with his best buddy, Foster Hyland, and a handful of their friends was beyond him. Clubs like this weren't his scene. Most of the guys he knew loved them, but watching women remove their clothes for a room full of strangers for money didn't do it for him. At least not since he'd been eighteen. At that age, all guys cared about was seeing tits and ass.

Making his way toward the main area with the tables, Max took a good look around. Almost all twenty or so tables, as well as every booth, were filled with drunk, rowdy onlookers. One large stage—with multiple poles reaching from floor to ceiling—and a DJ booth took up most of the east wall.

1

The waitresses moved slowly, as if they couldn't care less who got their drinks and who didn't, or it could be the ridiculously high heels they all wore. Someone whistled loudly over the booming music, catching Max's attention. He noticed his best friend waving to him from across the room. Two tables in the back had been pushed together to hold his party, and Max made his way over to where the other men were now standing to greet him.

Foster was the first to grab him in a manly shoulder hug. At six-foot-two, Foster was an inch shorter than Max. He still wore his sandy blond hair short on the sides, but it was longer on the top than it had been the last time they'd hung out a few weeks ago. That's when Foster had told him he was getting married.

"Glad you could make it." Foster had to raise his voice to be heard over the thumping beat.

Max grimaced. The music was already grating on his nerves. "I almost didn't. You're lucky I missed all your dumb asses."

Smiling, Max made the rounds, embracing the guys he knew and thought of as brothers while giving a polite hello to the few he didn't. The gang was all here tonight: Benjamin "Benji" Agani, Mortimer "Mother" Neville, Paxton "Tank" Sokolofski, Kasper "Gutter Mouth" Gutermuth, and Foster. Plus, the few guys Max didn't know made for a table of ten.

"For those of you who don't know, this is Max Fear," Foster announced, clapping Max on the back. "My best bud and personal 'Savior of my ass' on more than one occasion."

2

Max took a seat, with Foster on one side and Tank on the other. Ordering a beer from the waitress before she could scurry off again was harder than he thought it would be. The atmosphere sucked, but the company was what really mattered.

Tank turned toward him and grinned, his massive arms straining the thin cotton of his green t-shirt. With his buzz cut and olive skin, he looked like he'd just finished a tour overseas. "Max! Good to see you, man."

"It's been too long, Tank. How's that baby sister of yours?" Max teased, knowing damn well how protective Tank was over his little sister.

"A pain in the ass as always," Tank grumbled, shaking his head. "She pops in whenever she feels like it. Messes up my kitchen and leaves again."

Max raised his eyebrows. "She in town now?"

"Stay the fuck away from her." Tank bared his teeth, and Max burst out laughing.

The Boys in Blue back together again...Well, not all of them fell under that title anymore. Max had left the police force over a year ago. He hoped to open his own security firm, Fear Incorporated, in the near future. Gutter Mouth and Tank had retired two years before Max did. They were both doing private securities as well, only with different firms. Max hoped to poach them both once his business opened. He was close, but not quite there yet.

With a cold MGD in hand, he leaned back in the chair and listened to the guys tease and laugh around the tables. Taking a long pull off the bottle, one conversation caught his attention.

Across the table, a man with short blond hair

shook his head. "She's great, but she's so, I don't know...vanilla."

Foster stared unbelievingly at him. "Brody, I've heard stories of her and Mirabella. Are we talking about the same girl?"

Brody shrugged. "Whatever you've heard, I'm sure it was a lie. I don't even think she likes sex."

The waitress came back to refresh drinks. She was tall in her heels, with a strategically placed, tiny bikini covering her important bits. The fabric looked like foil, if foil were bright pink. She had great legs, probably from wearing ridiculous heels like that every night. Breasts like hers screamed silicone from across the room, and her hair was dyed to a bright candy apple red. Both her look and demeanor screamed cheap and easy. She stopped behind Brody, brushing her tits against the back of his shoulders.

"Comin' over tonight?" she purred.

Brody raised his eyebrows and grinned. "What time you off?"

"One."

"The boys and I should be done about that time."

"Great." She smiled before spinning around and running back to the bar with her empty tray.

Foster frowned. Max was sure he'd missed something being exchanged between the two of them. Whatever it was, his best friend looked disappointed and Brody looked indifferent. The guy was clearly a douchebag.

Foster narrowed his eyes. "Thought you stopped seeing Carmela?"

Brody winced. "I did...mostly." He reached up

4

to rub the back of his neck. "Aww hell, man. Don't look at me like that. A man has needs." Finally he had the good sense to look ashamed.

Max craned his neck to watch Carmela sashay over to another table. "Red over there isn't Ms. Vanilla, I take it?"

"Oh hell no," Brody blurted. "Ain't nothin' vanilla about Carm."

"So why are you with one girl when you want to be with another?" Benji questioned from the seat next to Brody.

"It's not right," Foster piped up.

"I gotta agree." Tank crossed his arms over his barrel chest, leaning back in his chair. He was clearly thinking of his own relationship, which had crashed and burned recently. She'd left him after admitting to a six-month affair just a few weeks ago. Around the table, most of the guys had stopped their conversations. Now they turned their attention to Brody.

"Sloane is gorgeous," Brody said. "Seriously hot. She's got her head on straight and she's the most responsible woman I know. I'm almost thirty-six; I need someone stable. Everything about her is amazing."

"I hear a 'but,'" Max said.

"But…She's cold. I have to initiate everything. Sex is mechanical. No matter how much I beg, I still can't get her to go down on me!"

All the guys started whooping and laughing then. Brody glared at all of them, but after a few minutes he just shook his head in defeat. Max never understood men like Brody. No relationship was perfect—that's why Max avoided them—but if you weren't getting what you needed, what was the point? Move on.

Foster frowned and folded his arms. "I can't lie to her again, Brody. I told you last time."

"Look, Foster, I know I've put you in a bad place with you marrying her cousin. Just tell her you didn't actually see me with anyone. Unless you're peepin' through windows, that's the truth anyway."

The cocky grin on Brody's face turned Max's stomach. Judging by Foster's expression, he felt the same disgust.

The crowd continued to cheer for the current topless dancer on stage, her slim body hanging upside down from one of the poles. Brody threw back another shot of amber liquid, never taking his eyes off the stage. He added his own catcalls to the mix. As much as Max loved his guys that were here, he couldn't stand looking at Brody for another minute. It was guys like him that made the rest of them look bad.

"I'm gonna bail, guys."

Foster threw his hands up. "Aww, Max, don't go yet."

"I gotta get some rest. I have a job in the morning."

"How about dinner? Mirabella's been asking when you're gonna come by again."

"Is she gonna make her famous beef stew?" Max raised an eyebrow in question, a big smile on his face.

Foster laughed. "I'm sure that can be arranged."

"Count me in. Call me tomorrow with a time and

I'll be there."

Max said his goodbyes and then made his way to the door. The fresh air slapped him in the face once he was out of the building, but it was refreshing after being inside. He headed for his truck on the other side of the parking lot, and once inside, clicked on the radio, turned on the headlights, and steered his truck toward his home on the outskirts of town. His nearest neighbor was a quarter mile away and he liked it like that.

Max pulled into the long driveway, coming to a stop behind the large farm-style house where the gravel path ended. The house had once belonged to his grandparents; when they'd gotten too old to care for it—and themselves—any longer, they'd sold it to Max for the bargain basement price of one dollar. He'd tried to pay them what it was worth, but his Granny smacked him good right in the back of the head and told him one day it would've gone to him anyway.

He was grateful for it every day. It gave him the means to quit the force when it no longer fit his ideals. For now, he worked for Winston Peters doing security and protection details. Funnily enough, his new job paid almost double, and without a house payment, Max was able to put a lot into his savings for the startup costs of his own business. His spare time, what little he had, was spent fixing up the old house. The front porch was beginning to show signs of rot, the kitchen needed an update, and the hardwood floors needed to be stripped and refurbished. Max walked in through the back door as always, toeing off his steel-toe boots in the laundry room before continuing into the kitchen for another beer.

He swallowed a third of the ice-cold brew in one sip while he moved through the house. By the time Max found himself in his bedroom, his beer was gone. Tossing the bottle in the trash can, he quickly brushed his teeth and washed his face. After stripping himself naked, Max crawled under the covers and stretched his arms up and behind his head. He needed to get some rest. Tomorrow was going to be a long day.

Chapter Two

Sloane

Sloane walked up the steps to her cousin Mirabella's house. Once again, she was attending their monthly Saturday night dinner alone. She understood Brody's job was important, but she had a hard time understanding how he could never get away when Foster, Mirabella's fiancé, almost always made it on time. Sadly, she was beginning to get used to being the third wheel.

She should've just cancelled, but the idea of sitting home alone—again—was more depressing than attending dinner by herself. She knocked loudly, and without waiting for a reply, she walked inside.

"Bella?"

"Kitchen," Mirabella called out.

Sloane practically floated into the kitchen, following the savory smell. Mirabella was bent over checking the food in the oven. She looked like she'd been pulled from the page of a 1950's magazine. Her long blonde hair was pulled up in a stylish twist, and an A-line dress in black and white that had a red sash cinched around her slender waist ended just above her knees. Red pumps that seemed silly to Sloane—who wore heels in her own house?—completed her look.

"Oh my...Is that your famous stew?" Sloane practically had to wipe the drool off her bottom lip. Her stomach growled as she breathed in the savory smell.

After closing the oven door, Mirabella turned to her, smiling. "Yes, it is." Her smile faded a little. "Where's Brody?"

"Work...You know..."

Bella shook her head. "Yeah, I know. Grab that bottle of wine over there and pour us a glass, Chickie."

"Where's Foster? I can't believe he isn't in here trying to sneak food when your back is turned." She chuckled.

"I heard that." Foster entered the kitchen looking relaxed in a pair of black jeans and a red button-down shirt. He crossed the room and kissed Sloane on the cheek. "How ya doin', Hon?"

"Not too bad. My boss has been forgetting things again, so my job has been that much harder trying to make up for it. I've had to make excuses for so many missed meetings, but I'm not sure what else I can do."

Being the personal assistant to Detlef Marek, CEO of Marek Enterprises, was definitely a challenge some days. Lately it was downright exhausting. His company had its fingers in multiple pies. From real estate to insurance to construction—

you name it, Mr. Marek had an interest in it. He was a decent enough guy, and even in his mid-fifties, he was still a captivating man. Thankfully he wasn't a pervert like her last boss had been, and unlike his son, Sydney. Sydney Marek was every bit as charming as his father when he wanted to be. Unfortunately, he didn't want to very often.

After gathering the side dishes, Sloane carried them to the dining room table, where she saw the fourth setting that would be a symbol of Brody's absence the entire night. Maybe she should clear the setting before they sat down. Sighing, she headed back to the kitchen, only to change courses to answer the extremely loud doorbell.

"Got it," she called over her shoulder.

Maybe Brody had gotten away from work after all. Quickening her stride, she couldn't help but feel excited at the prospect of Brody surprising her. Her disappointment was short lived, however. She pulled the door open, and standing on the front porch was a man that she'd never seen before.

He was tall with shaggy brown hair that fell over his forehead and the tops of his ears. Eyes the color of strong whiskey—whiskey she'd gladly get drunk on—were framed by the darkest eyelashes she had ever seen without help from mascara. The three-day-old stubble on his face only added to the allure, and she could see the hint of a tattoo peeking out below his shirtsleeve.

"Hello," she croaked. "Can I help you?"

His gaze skimmed down her body quickly before flicking back up to meet her eyes. "Hi, I'm looking for Foster or Mirabella."

"Great. You're just in time," Foster called as he closed the distance between them. "Come on in, man."

"It smells like Heaven in here." The stranger brushed past Sloane and shook Foster's hand.

Foster gestured toward her. "Max, this is Sloane, Bella's cousin."

"Nice to meet you," Max said courteously, offering his hand. A small grin tugged at his full, kissable lips.

Sloane shook his hand, nodding politely before following the men back to the dining room, sneaking glances at Max the whole time. The man had the finest ass to ever be encased in a pair of denim. Mmmm. Good grief, what was wrong with her? A long dry spell was what was wrong. Brody hadn't so much as touched her in the last few months. Sadly, it didn't bother her as much as it should; he had gotten increasingly more aggressive during sex, causing more pain than pleasure. She hadn't had an orgasm the last dozen or so times they were together. She'd rather go without at this point. How depressing was that? Sloane poured another glass of wine for herself, downing half before taking a seat. Max took the seat across from her, leaving the other two seats for Bella and Foster.

"Bella, I've been dreaming of this all week." Max winked at her.

Bella laughed. "Glad you could finally drag your ass over here. It's been too long," she scolded playfully.

"Yes, it has."

"How's the job?"

"Eh, I've been running backgrounds mostly this week."

Bella smiled. "Didn't I see you in the paper last week? The society page to boot."

"Yeah, I was keeping a watch on Yancy Bloodworth's daughter, Zoë. It was her twenty-third birthday. Daddy didn't want anyone getting too 'handsy' with his little princess." He rolled his eyes.

"As in Yancy Bloodworth, real estate mogul?" Sloane asked, filling her glass again. Mirabella gave her a sideways glance, making a point to look at her very full glass. Sloane just shrugged a shoulder at her.

Max nodded. "I do security, among other things. He hired me to keep her safe."

"Mr. Bloodworth is an intimidating guy. He's not very big physically, but there's something about him that sets my teeth on edge."

Max's eyebrows shot up. "You know him?" He seemed surprised. Sloane wasn't sure why that bothered her.

"I'm Detlef Marek's personal assistant; they have dealings together and he often comes by the office."

The four of them made small talk until they finished dinner. Sloane helped Mirabella clear the table and get dessert. She took all the plates in first, returning to collect the wine glasses. Max handed over his, their fingertips touching briefly. His eyes locked with hers. She could feel the heat that colored her cheeks as she spun around, quickly retreating to the kitchen.

"I'll pour the coffee," she muttered.

13

"You all right, Sloane? You look flushed." Bella smirked.

"I'm fine. Must be the wine. Why are you looking at me like that?"

"It could be the wine, or…It could be that fine example of a man out there."

"Max? I don't even know him."

"But you want to."

"Shut up, Bella. Even if I did want to, I'm already seeing someone."

"Look, I mean this in the most loving way: You are a moron."

Sloane narrowed her eyes. "Excuse me?"

"Brody is a piece of shit if I ever met one, and you deserve a whole hell of a lot better."

Mirabella stood on the other side of the kitchen island with her hands on her hips, her expression daring Sloane to disagree. Mirabella was more than her cousin—she was her best friend. Denying Brody's affairs would be pointless since Sloane had cried on Bella's couch just last month and it hadn't been the first time. She had a feeling he was up to his old tricks again, but she wasn't going to admit that to Bella.

"We've had our roadblocks, yeah."

"Roadblocks? That's what you call finding him in bed with a stripper? A stripper, Sloane."

Sloane's eyes burned; she couldn't go down that road right now. It was too much. "I don't want to talk about it tonight, Bella," she whispered. "Please."

"Oh, honey, I'm sorry." She walked around the island and took Sloane in her arms. "It just pisses

14

me off that he thinks he can do that to you."

"I know." Her whispered words hung between them for a moment. Sloane knew that he thought he could do those things because she always forgave him. She also knew she should leave him, only she wasn't strong enough to actually do it. She kept hoping he would change.

"All right," Bella said. "Grab some plates. I've got the pie."

***

Max

Max looked up as the women came out of the kitchen. The smell of warm cherry pie filled the room. Biting into his slice, Max tried to keep his gaze from traveling over to Sloane. She was breathtaking. When she'd opened the front door, he'd thought he might have to pick up his lower jaw before he walked into the house. Her skin was ivory and looked softer than satin. He loved that she wasn't artificially tanned like a lot of women he encountered in his line of work. Her honey-colored hair was loose, hanging halfway down her back. Max longed to fist his hands in it. The thought tightened his pants. *Shit.* He had to calm down. No way she wouldn't notice if he had to stand anytime soon.

Sloane's phone rang. Smiling at the screen, she quickly excused herself and hurried into the kitchen. Foster shook his head, and Mirabella gave him a small, sad half smile. Sloane's raised voice floated in from the kitchen. They all sat quietly, trying not to be obvious about the fact they were all trying to eavesdrop. Bella worried her bottom lip, stealing glances at Foster. Foster alternated his gaze between Bella and the kitchen door. They were failing miserably at it. Max watched them quietly, wondering what could be going on to cause the concerned expression on Bella's face. Suddenly it all became clear.

"Why not? You promised you wouldn't miss tonight, Brody...Selfish? Me? ...who is she this time? I know you're fucking someone! I'm not stupid! ...Whatever. Do what you want. You always do."

Sloane came out of the kitchen with a fresh bottle of red wine in one hand and a glass in the other. "Sorry about that, what did I miss?"

She smiled, only this time it didn't reach her expressive blue eyes. While Mirabella was completely put together even for an evening at home, her nails freshly painted and every hair in its proper place, Sloane was the opposite. Her polish was starting to chip, bangs that were slightly overgrown framed her face, and she wore a simple V-neck t-shirt with blue jeans. She was exactly what Max liked. She sat down, looking at Bella expectantly.

"We were just discussing going to Velvet Ropes next weekend. Are you in?"

Damn, Bella lied good. Max chuckled to himself. Velvet Ropes was the newest club to open its doors. The line to get in was always wrapped halfway around the building after eight at night, even on weekdays. Max had been there once for a job.

Sloane smoothed her hair from her face. "Sure, why not. I doubt I'll have plans."

"Max, you said you were in, right?" Mirabella smiled slyly.

"How could I refuse after you made stew?"

"You can't."

The next thing Max knew it was almost midnight. Sloane's bottle of red was as empty as her glass. The alcohol induced pink flush covering her cheeks made him smile to himself, even if the reason she drank that much didn't. This was Brody's "vanilla" girlfriend—the one he was cheating on, and apparently not for the first time.

The three of them had settled in the living room after dinner, and he now sat in the recliner in the corner, watching Sloane stare into the fireplace. Mirabella and Foster held hands on the couch, whispering into each other's ear. They occasionally glanced at Sloane, only to whisper some more. Sometimes giggling, but mostly they looked concerned.

Max couldn't take his eyes off her; she made his insides crawl. It was as though his skin was too tight for his body. He wanted to push her hair out of her eyes like he'd watched her do a dozen times tonight. He wanted to tell her Brody was a damn fool and didn't deserve her. To take her lips with his. He wanted her. Plain and simple. But he'd just met her. How could he feel this strongly? It didn't make any sense.

Sloane stood up abruptly like she'd awakened from a trance. She staggered slightly, using the mantel to steady herself.

"Thank you both for dinner," she said. "It's late; I better get going."

Bella shook her head. "Honey, stay here tonight. You're in no condition to drive."

"I'm fine, really." She stumbled, only to fling a hand out to balance against the wall.

Max stood up. "I'll take her home. I was going to head out myself."

"That's all right, Max. You don't have to," Bella protested.

Max walked over to Sloane and gently pried her keys from her fingers. Warmth spread from every place her fingers touched his. It radiated up his arm and throughout his body similar to an electric current from a live wire. She pulled her hand back quickly, her eyes widening. Max knew she felt it too. His eyes were drawn to her full lips, and her tongue darted across them, leaving them glistening. His body responded to such a simple act just as easily as if she'd rubbed herself against him. Yup, time to get outta here before Foster figured it out. He always could read Max like a book.

"Don't even think about it," Max said. "I'm driving, no arguments."

"Aren't we bossy?" she mumbled under her breath.

They said their goodbyes. Max hugged Mirabella, making sure to keep the lower half of his body pulled away from her. Last thing he needed was for her to know he was semi-erect. Foster raised an eyebrow and smirked. He gave Max's shoulder a slap goodbye. *Shit*. He knew something was going on.

Sloane trailed him out of the house to his pick-up truck parked on the street. He opened her door, making sure she was settled inside the cabin before closing it. Max walked around the front of the truck and slid in the driver's seat.

"Thank you," Sloane murmured. "I don't normally drink so much when I know I have to drive."

"Don't mention it. There are worse things to do besides escorting a beautiful woman home."

Sloane gave him directions across town to her apartment building. He parked in the only empty spot he could find. Taking her hand, Max helped her out of the vehicle. He was reluctant to let her go, but he did. Not trusting his ability to keep his hands to himself, he shoved his hands in his pockets, and they walked toward the building side by side. The moon was full overhead, illuminating the parking lot. Once inside, she stopped in front of the elevators. She leaned against the wall after pushing the Up button.

"I'm on the fifth floor. Apartment five-oh-four." She reiterated the apartment number with her fingers, drawing it in the air with a giggle that sent a jolt down his spine.

Shaking his head and trying to hide his own smile, he took her by the elbow to lead her inside the elevator car. Max pushed the button marked with a five. The doors closed and the car rose quickly. She slumped against the back wall of the car.

Max imagined what she might taste like. He

could easily fantasize stalking over to where she stood and pinning her to the wall as he claimed her lips. He stood there watching her until the doors reopened on her floor. After guiding her down the hallway, he stood outside her apartment door and waited for her to unlock it and enter before he left. She turned to him with the door partially open.

"Thanks again, Max."

Her big blue eyes looked up at him from under those damn bangs. Without thinking what a gigantic mistake it was, Max gave in and slowly pushed her bangs away from her face. Those beautiful blues stole the small amount of resistance he had left. He slid his hand around the back of her neck, pulling her to him and claiming her lips. He slanted his mouth across hers, pulling a small moan from her. His tongue slipped past her lips and caressed hers. She tasted of cherries and red wine. Sloane pulled him even closer using his belt loops as handles, pressing her hips into him. His erect cock pressed into her tender belly. He was coming unglued. How could one kiss light him on fire like this?

Sloane pulled back, gasping, when her phone started ringing. Her trembling fingers touched her kiss-swollen lips in…shock? Perhaps awe?

"I should get that," she panted. Every macho-infused cell in his body relished the knowledge that he made her do that. She was just as affected as he was.

"Don't," he said sternly. Her eyes widened, but otherwise she didn't move a muscle. Max closed the narrow space between them yet again. Sloane's breath hitched before his lips crashed down on hers.

He released her abruptly. "I better go."

Max kissed her forehead softly. Turning quickly, he made his way a few feet back to the elevator doors. He looked back while he waited for the steel doors to open.

"And Sloane, next time you even think of driving home after drinking and I hear about it, there *will* be consequences."

Sloane still stood in the doorway of her apartment, her gaze glued to his. Her phone, temporarily forgotten in her hand, hung by her side. Did she know it was still ringing?

Chapter Three

Sloane

Barely able to breathe, Sloane slipped inside and closed the door. She looked down at the phone that kept ringing in her hand. Brody. She *so* wasn't in the mood to speak to him. Not only had he blown her off again, but after those scorching kisses from Max, there was no way she was in the right frame of mind to deal with him. Hitting the Ignore button, she quickly sent a text to Mirabella. She let her know that she had arrived home safely and would be by tomorrow to get her car.

Without waiting for her reply, Sloane grabbed a t-shirt to sleep in. Once it was on, she smelled Brody. Eyeing herself in the mirror, the oversized t-shirt mocked her. No way was she wearing his shirt while Max invaded her every thought. She wondered what consequences he could be talking about. Her body involuntarily shivered. She pulled off the t-shirt and threw it into the hamper before she climbed into bed.

The next morning came way too soon. Sloane needed a carafe of coffee and half a bottle of aspirin, at the very least. She fetched a clean t-shirt—one of her own—and a pair of yoga pants. She needed to go find deliverance from the polka band playing in her head. Ugh, why oh why did she drink so much last night?

After making it slowly to the living room, she decided coffee was in order first. She veered to the left, entering her kitchen nook, and fumbled to set the coffee up. The smell teased her senses. A long gong tore her attention away from the little miracle machine percolating in front of her. She hurried to get to the front hall before the doorbell rang again. Too late—the sound pulled a groan from her and she covered her ears like a toddler. The clock on the microwave showed it was just after eight. Who could that be this early on a Sunday? Peeking through the peephole suspiciously, she almost started to drool. Standing on the other side of her door, looking like a god, was Max. She took a moment to appreciate him this way, rather than to gawk openly where he could see.

His sunglasses were perched on top of his head. He still hadn't shaved. Normally she went for the clean-cut, boy-next-door look, but for some reason the shaggy hair and stubble turned her insides into putty. His gaze landed right on the small glass circle she was looking out of. The corner of his lip pulled up into a small smirk. The sight caused her pulse to speed up.

"I'm not leaving, so you might as well open the door, Sloane."

Oh. My. God! Sloane quickly backed away from the door. How did he…? Taking a deep cleansing breath, she reached forward, unlocked the door, and pulled it open. Max drank her in openly. Every place his eyes landed ignited as if he had actually touched her.

"How did you know I was there?"

"I could see your shadow under the door. I figured you were watching for me to give up and leave. Not likely."

"Oh. What are you doing here?"

"I thought you could use a lift back to Foster's to get your car. I was heading there anyway."

"Thank you for thinking of me. I still need to get dressed; I don't want to hold you up."

"We have plenty of time. I can wait…that is, unless you take as long as Bella to get ready." He laughed.

"Good grief, no! I love her and all, but that girl makes getting ready look like an Olympic event. It'll only take me about twenty minutes. Come on inside and make yourself comfortable."

Sloane opened the door wider to allow Max to enter her apartment. She tried not to sniff him. She really did.

"Okay. Thanks."

She led him into the kitchen area where the smell of brewed coffee made her salivate.

"Would you mind if I finished my coffee first, though? I don't think it would be wise for anyone to be around me if I didn't get my caffeine fix."

"Not at all."

"Thanks, would you like some?"

24

"Sure. Just black, please."

Sloane filled another mug with coffee and placed it in front of Max. She stood on one side of the little kitchen island as he sat on a stool across from her. She watched him sip from his mug. She loved the way his large hand wrapped around it, instead of using the handle. He glanced around the room, taking in her apartment. No other men had been in her apartment other than Brody or Foster in ages, and she didn't know what to say to Max. Luckily he saved her from stumbling through an icebreaker.

"Nice place. Lived here long?"

"Almost five years."

"Have you worked for Detlef long?"

"I've been his assistant for three years now. How about you—how long have you been a bodyguard?"

Bodyguard. She devoured him with her eyes. His t-shirt hugged his shoulders and chest in the most delicious way. She wanted to see more of the tattoos that disappeared under his shirt. Her mind started to wander. *He can guard my body whenever he wa— Oh God.* Where had *that* thought come from? She shouldn't be picturing him pressed up against her, but now all she could think about was him pinning her against the fridge, that stubbled jaw grazing against her neck…Heat crawled up her face. Hopefully Max didn't notice. The way he was currently studying her however, there was no way he didn't notice. He tried to hide a smirk. She was totally busted. Ugh.

"I'm not really a bodyguard, per se. I do private securities. The actual tasks vary per client. I got into it last year after I left the force."

"That sounds exciting." She didn't know exactly what that meant. However, she bet he looked sexy as hell doing it.

After a few more minutes of small talk, Sloane excused herself to take a very cold shower. She needed the distance to get herself under control. Never before had she wanted to run her hands over a man the way she wanted to with Max. Everything about him called to her. She had to continuously keep reminding herself what a bad idea it would be to run back out to wrap herself around him while licking every inch of his body. She stepped under the frigid spray and squealed. Holy shit was it cold.

"Are you all right?"

Max's voice boomed from just outside the bathroom door. She shrieked, jumped, and lost her balance. She tried to regain her footing, but the slick shower floor had her scrambling to keep herself upright. Her effort, however, was in vain—she slipped and landed hard on her ass.

It wouldn't have been so bad if her elbow and head hadn't also connected with the side and back of the tub. She groaned as she lay there. Both embarrassment and pride kept her from getting up immediately.

The bathroom door flung open. Max rushed to her side, grabbing her fluffy pink towel from the counter on the way.

He turned off the cold water that had been streaming over her head. He picked her up and wrapped the towel around her quickly. Max made her step over the side and sat her on the toilet lid. Sloane's teeth hadn't stopped chattering, even though she was out from under the glacial spray. Wrapping her arms around herself tightly, she tried to warm herself. Max knelt in front of her, rubbing his warm, calloused hands up and down her arms and creating a mouthwatering friction, heating her skin wherever his hands were…and some places they weren't.

"Damn, woman," he barked. "Are you trying to give me a heart attack?"

She merely looked at him in response. His eyes were wild, worry etched into them. The poor man's clothes were wrinkled and had wet patches all over them from when he had picked her up.

He had the best lips ever. Sloane was tempted to lean over and lick them to see if they tasted as good as they did last night. He stopped rubbing her arms. The loss of heat pulled a whimper past her lips. He took her chin in his hand, studying her face as he tenderly touched the throbbing spot on the back of her head.

"Thankfully you don't seem to have done much damage, but you're gonna have quite the knot and a mother of a headache."

"Already had the headache," she murmured with a grimace.

"Come on, I'll help you to your room."

Something flashed in Max's eyes before his body went rigid. He took a visible breath, then closed his eyes as he motioned to her. Glancing down, Sloane found her towel had slipped down far enough to show a *lot* of cleavage and part of her left nipple. Oh my God! Max had just gotten an eyeful of her breast. Come to think of it, he'd pulled her out of the tub. Max had seen *every* part of her naked. Buck fucking naked. Sloane was mortified.

"Oh. My. God. I'm so sorry, Max!"

She pulled the traitorous towel up, securing it better as she stood. Too bad it left a lot of leg showing that way, but at least it covered everything important.

"You're sorry?" He cracked an eye open to verify that she was now decent. "I should apologize for bursting in, but I was afraid you knocked yourself out when you didn't answer me."

"Thank you. I'm…I'm gonna go get dressed. I'll be out in a few minutes."

Sloane raced past him, locking the bedroom door behind her. More to keep herself in than to keep him out. After opening her panty drawer, she stopped and stared. What color would get Max's undivided attention? She groaned at her stupidity. She didn't need to think about the sexiness that was Max. She needed to figure out what to do about her failing relationship with Brody.

She grabbed a pair of panties at random and the matching bra. After she was finished getting dressed in jeans and a tight t-shirt, she pulled her hair back and secured it with an elastic band. Except for her bangs—they were too short to reach the tie. Without a need to impress the sexy man that had already seen her drunk, hung over, and now naked in a heap at the bottom of her bathtub, she quickly put on some mascara and went to Max.

***

Max

Maybe he should ask her to use her shower. He needed an ice cold one to control his cock; it pushed against his zipper painfully. He'd barely registered her naked in the tub, he was so worried about her. It wasn't until he was checking to see if she had broken anything or split anything open that he'd noticed her towel had fallen enough to reveal one perfectly pink nipple. He wanted to lower his head and take the bud between his lips.

He walked out of her bathroom, unsuccessfully brushing the wrinkles from his shirt while making his way back to the kitchen. Once he'd stepped around the corner, he found Brody looking down at the kitchen table. Confusion painted his face at the sight of not one, but two mugs of coffee. His head snapped up when he heard Max's footsteps.

"What the hell are you doing here?"

"What are *you* doing here?" Max answered. Better to let him think he didn't know Sloane was this tool bag's girlfriend.

"This is my girlfriend's place."

"Sloane is your girlfriend?"

The look on Brody's face was a combination of uncertainty and anger. But Max was saved from further inquisition—just then Sloane strode in brushing her bangs from her eyes again.

"Thanks again, Max, I know you weren't expecting—" She looked up and screeched to a stop. "Brody?"

"Sloane. What the hell is Max doing here?"

"You know each other?" She looked like she was

about to hyperventilate. All the color drained from her face. Max wanted to wipe that look off of her face.

"We met the other night, hanging out with Foster." Max spoke calmly. No telling what this looked like to Brody. Max still had wet spots on his shirt and Sloane obviously had just gotten out of the shower. Add the two cups of coffee and the early hour, and it probably looked like Max had spent the night. Would serve him right. Brody was cheating on her and it sounded like it was nothing new.

What was worse though, was that from Sloane's phone conversation last night, she knew all about it and still stayed with him. Couldn't she see this relationship was toxic? She needed a man who knew how to take care of his woman.

"I came by this morning to give Sloane a ride. She was a little too tipsy to drive home last night."

Brody gave her an accusing look. Hypocrite. "I thought you were at Foster's last night for dinner? Where the hell were you?"

"I was!"

Max narrowed his eyes. "I was there too. Foster invited me, and good thing too. She'd needed someone to look after her to get home safe."

"Oh, well I can drive you, sweetheart. Thanks for making sure my girl got home, Max."

Brody smiled, but the look reminded Max of a snake. His entire demeanor changed. He slithered over to where Sloane stood and wrapped his arms around her, nuzzling her neck. Max felt jealousy well up inside him. He wanted to drill that asshole in the face before plunging his tongue in Sloane's mouth. He wanted to take her in his arms and show her why she should be with him instead of that dick head. He needed to claim her as his. *Whoa.* Where did that come from? Max counted backward from five before he felt controlled enough to speak.

"Sure thing. I'll just be going then since you've got a ride. See ya around, Sloane. Later, man."

Max acknowledged Brody with a nod before he turned, letting himself out of Sloane's apartment.

Chapter Four

Sloane

Sloane sat in the passenger seat of Brody's car with her hands in her lap. Her gaze stayed fixed out the side window, watching the streets speed by. It was strange and yet exciting to see a man so concerned about her well-being. Max had rushed in to help and it warmed her inside more than she wanted to admit. She was shocked when she found Brody in her kitchen only minutes after being naked with Max...okay, so she hadn't been naked in the way she wanted to be, but naked all the same.

Sloane wanted Max, but knew she couldn't have him. She was committed to Brody. Plus, she was certain Max had no shortage of women falling all over him, so she wouldn't stand a chance. She didn't want another relationship that she had to compete to stay in.

"Look, I'm sorry I missed dinner last night. Let me make it up to you tonight. Dinner, maybe a little dancing, it'll be nice. Then we can go back to my place."

"Back to my place" always meant sex. Over the course of their relationship the sex had usually been good, but he cared more about his own pleasure than he did about his partner. He was a selfish lover. Still, Sloane cared about him. She sighed.

She'd met him on a blind double date with Foster and Bella. He'd been incredibly charming and easy on the eyes, with his short, dark blond hair and pale green eyes. He wasn't very tall for a man, but his charisma more than made up for it. He'd swept her off her feet, and in return, she'd tried to be everything he wanted.

But he always wanted her to go down on him. She'd been ashamed to admit to him that she'd never done that before. Sure, she'd had other lovers, but none she felt comfortable enough to experience that with. She was more conservative when it came to sex, but he'd seemed okay with that at the start of their relationship.

Brody had looked like a kid in a candy store when she'd told him he would be her first. His excitement had fueled her own at first. But Sloane had barely had her lips around him when he fisted her hair painfully and thrust himself down her throat. The forcefulness and depth caused her throat to burn and her gag reflex to go into overdrive. Vomiting all over him wasn't the way she had planned to end the evening. He'd left pissed off and she'd spent the rest of the night alone, crying herself to sleep. Never again.

It wasn't long after that when she'd caught him in bed with another woman. He'd said it was just sex. He needed someone to do the things she wouldn't. That he loved her and wouldn't do it again. Knowing it was all bullshit, Sloane still couldn't bring herself to end it. It was her fault after all. She wasn't a good enough lover for him.

"It's Sunday. I have to finish up a spreadsheet for Mr. Marek and be in early tomorrow."

"I try to make it right and you shut me out," he spat, shaking his head. "Typical."

"I'm sorry, Brody. Mondays are crazy. It helps if I get in earlier than Mr. Marek so I can have things ready for his arrival."

"Why can't you see to my needs like you see to his every fuckin' whim?"

"Because he's my boss and that's what he pays me for," Sloane yelled right back.

It seemed like every conversation had ended in an argument the past few months. She was sick and tired of it. Why couldn't she have a relationship like her cousin, Mirabella? Bella had a great man in Foster. Loyal, thoughtful, and dependable. He never forced her to do anything. They were getting married in a few weeks and they seemed more in love each day. She could admit she was jealous. She wanted that for herself. The happiness that came with a man who was truly in love with you. She pictured Max. The way his eyes danced when he'd laughed at dinner last night. The thought added to the warmth low in her belly. He came across as the type of man who made it his mission to ruin a woman for all other men. Sloane involuntarily shivered just thinking about him.

"Don't tell me you're cold? It's hot as hell in

here."

Sloane didn't bother answering. They had arrived at Bella's house, finally. As soon as he put the car in park, she opened the door, quickly getting out. It was horrible, but she couldn't wait to be away from him. That should've told her something right there.

Brody's door opened. Cautiously, she turned around at the top of the stairs on the front porch. He stood by the open car door with his arms crossed over the hood. Great, show time. Mentally, she rolled her eyes.

"Have a great time, sweetheart," he called, talking loud enough for everyone inside to hear him. "I'll call you later. We'll finally have that alone time that we need." He winked before folding himself back into his car to drive away.

Just what she needed. As she was trekking into the house, she noticed Max's truck parked across the street in the same spot it had been last night. Sighing, she walked inside. *Lovely.* Bella was sitting at the dining room table with Foster hunched over her from behind. His arms were crossed over Bella's shoulders. They were laughing. They were so happy, it almost made Sloane's heart break for her own shitty relationship. Across from the happy couple sat Max.

"Hi, guys." Sloane tried to sound chipper even though her headache from the morning was doing its best to creep back up.

Foster stood up and began marching toward her. He picked her up and spun her around once before setting her feet back on the floor. He had treated her like family from the first day they met. She had instantly liked him.

Bella sat smiling over what she could now see were wedding invitations. Max sat back in his chair stretching one arm over the back. The move put his expansive chest on display. She could make out more of the tattoo swirls on his arm. She had to drag her eyes away from him before she actually drooled on herself. The man was like sex on a stick and she wanted to lick every inch of him. Slowly and thoroughly.

Foster folded his arms, throwing her a mock glare. "You can pretend to be cheery all you want, Robertson, but we know better."

"I don't know what you're babbling about, Hyland. I'm just fine."

"Whenever a woman describes herself as 'fine,' she's anything but." He laughed.

Foster was a bit of a goof, but God love him, he knew how to lighten a room up. Sloane wandered over to Bella and kissed her cheek. They were more like sisters than cousins and best friends as long as either of them could remember.

"Maid of Honor reporting for duty." Sloane's smile was overenthusiastic. Feeling eyes on her, she turned her head. "Hey, Max."

"Sloane."

She loved her name on his lips. The way he'd said it in the past was more than just a name. It sounded like a promise. This time however, it sounded darker. Almost guarded. It shouldn't affect her this way. It shouldn't matter how he said her name. Not before and not now. It did, though. She couldn't take her traitorous eyes from him. He didn't even blink—just met the stare until she turned away. She had to break the connection. It was too much and yet not enough.

Sloane cleared her throat. "So, it looks like invitations are on the agenda today."

"That's right," Bella chirped. "Grab one of those pens and here's one half of the guest list. Want a Bloody Mary or a Screwdriver?"

"God no! Not after last night."

Mirabella snorted with laughter. Sloane rolled her eyes, but couldn't hold back her own chuckle. She risked a peek across the table from where she'd taken a seat, and her eyes locked once again with Max's. He slowly shook his head for a moment before standing up to take a seat in the living room. He wasn't acting like the guy she'd met last night. Did she do something wrong? More importantly, why did it matter?

Bella glanced up from filling out the address on a cream envelope. "What's going on with Brody? I heard him outside earlier."

"He wants to make it up to me for missing dinner. He got stuck at work."

Bella scoffed. "We both know that's bullshit."

"Bella..."

"Don't 'Bella' me! You're my family and I love you. I can't stand watching him hurt you over and over and you just take it. You make excuses and defend him. What the hell, Sloane?"

"It's not his fault!" Sloane yelled back. Humiliation colored her face. Mirabella didn't know she didn't measure up to what Brody wanted in the bedroom. He wanted someone adventurous. He wanted someone to do things that she wasn't comfortable doing, and when she resisted that's when things had begun to change. That's when *he* changed. There's no way Bella would understand.

"Ladies—" Foster marched into the room. "Enough. Bella, sweetheart, as much as I agree with you, this isn't our decision. It's Sloane's."

"Thank you," Sloane whispered.

"Oh no. Don't go thanking me yet. You need to get your head outta your ass and realize we only want you happy. Before you try to interrupt me and lie, we both know you aren't."

Sloane cast her eyes down, not wanting to meet his gaze. They both loved her. She knew that, but it wasn't the same as having someone to hold at night. To chase away the fears and show her there were better days ahead. They had that.

"All right, Max and I are gonna head out. Don't scratch up any furniture with your cat fights." He winked again and headed for the living room where Max had sat silently listening to the whole conversation. Now she *really* felt like an ass. Great.

***

Max

How could cheating on her not be Brody's fault? Max couldn't wrap his mind around that. Unless she told him to go fuck around, it didn't make sense. The conversation—which he'd made no attempt to ignore—between her and Mirabella inclined him to

38

believe she knew about more than one indiscretion. Maybe Foster could enlighten him a bit.

"What's the story with those two?"

Foster sighed. "They've been seeing each other for about a year. He's been screwing around almost as long. I try not to get involved, but Sloane is a sweet girl. She's family. Even though I don't volunteer information, if she asks me, I won't lie either."

"I get that. What I don't get is why she stays. She's beautiful. She seems smart and funny. Why waste her time with him when she could do better?"

Foster glanced over at him, a small grin lifting the corner of his mouth. Max tried to act like he didn't notice. They rode in silence for a few miles before Foster had to press.

"Are you throwing your hat in the ring?"

"What are you talking about?" Max snapped.

"Sloane. You have a thing for her." Foster laughed.

He had a thing for her, all right. Every time they were in the same room, he had to stop himself from touching her. After seeing Brody's arm around her this morning, he'd wanted to throw her down and cover her with his body. Leaving only his scent on her. *What the fuck.* He wasn't some kind of animal. He needed to stop thinking of her that way. She was off limits.

But as much as he tried, he couldn't stop thinking of the kiss they'd shared in the hallway of her building. Brody called her cold at the strip club, but he couldn't reconcile the woman Brody spoke about with Sloane. She was so hot; he'd felt like he would burn up in flames when his tongue met hers.

"Earth to Max."

"Huh? Oh, it's a shame."

"Oh yeah, you're interested."

"Fuck you, man."

"That much, huh?" Foster cackled with uncontrollable laughter.

"You're a dick. You know that?"

"That I do."

When Max walked into work Monday morning, he cursed under his breath. Zoë Youngblood stood outside his office door with her entourage.

She flashed him the thousand-watt smile that she'd perfected for the cameras always following her around. This couldn't be good. "Maxwell Fear. Just the man I'd wanted to see."

"Ms. Youngblood, how can I help you?"

"Please call me Zoë. You make me feel like an old maid. Do I look like a frumpy old maid to you, Max?"

She sauntered up to him and dragged a bright red, manicured nail down his bicep. The other hand slid seductively down her hip. Whatever she was fishing for, he wasn't biting.

"What do you want, Ms. Youngblood?"

"You're no fun, Max." Pouting, she crossed her arms under her breasts, trying to push them up so he would take notice.

"I'm a busy man."

"I was thinking of taking a trip and Daddy said I needed a bodyguard. So I thought to myself, 'Zoë *dah*-ling. Who would be best suited to guard your body?' Only one man came to mind. So here I am."

"Thank you for the confidence, but I'm sorry, I can't."

"You can't?" She seemed appalled by his refusal.

"I have other clients. I only take local jobs."

His statement was bullshit. The only jobs Max had at this moment could easily be completed from anywhere in the world that had Wi-Fi. But no way was he going to tell her that. He didn't want to be involved in any way with Zoë Youngblood, especially not with all the signals she was throwing out.

"Money's no object."

"I can't be bought," he said. She laughed at him, and he gritted his teeth.

"*Anyone* can be bought. All you have to do is find their price."

Zoë spun on her ridiculous heels and sashayed to the elevator. Her slim hips swayed with blatant exaggeration. Most men would probably fall to her feet begging, but not Max. He liked his women curvier. A certain curvy blonde came to mind. He smiled to himself as he made his way over to his office.

After pushing the door open, he walked over and plopped into his oversized leather office chair. Hopefully work could distract him enough to keep images of Sloane from his mind. *Yeah, good luck with that*, he mocked himself.

Chapter Five

Sloane

Sloane couldn't believe she'd almost worked right through lunchtime. The morning was filled with appointments, conference calls, and errands. If she hadn't set a reminder on the calendar to pick up Mr. Marek's dry cleaning during her lunch, she wouldn't have remembered to even take a lunch today. Shutting the computer down, she smoothed out her pencil skirt before tapping gently on the boss's door.

"Come in."

"Sir, I'm heading out for lunch. I'll have your suits with me when I return."

"Thank you, Sloane. You are a lifesaver."

"Thank you, sir. Is there anything else I can get you while I'm out?"

"No, I think you do enough for me as it is." He smiled warmly.

"I'll be back within the hour. Don't forget you're meeting with Mr. Peters at two o'clock."

Taking the elevator down to the ground floor, she exited the building out of the side door. It was only three blocks to the dry cleaners, but in her heels, there was no way she was walking. Not when she would be carrying lunch, plus hangers full of heavy suits. Once in her car and on the road, she turned toward Maple Drive. As usual, the dry cleaner had the clothes ready when she walked in.

Gathering the suits in her arms, she darted into the deli next door to order a turkey sandwich to take back with her. The smell of fresh bread assaulted her nose, making her stomach rumble. Impatiently, she waited for her number to be called. It was already one-thirty when she walked out of the small deli. Since she wanted to have herself settled before Mr. Peters arrived, she knew she'd have to hurry.

The elevator dinged before opening on the floor housing Mr. Marek's office. Sloane had twenty minutes to hang up his weekly suits in his office closet and scarf the food down. She scurried to her desk, dropped the sandwich off, and immediately pushed open Mr. Marek's door.

The first thing that came into view was Detlef Marek, kneeling on the floor in front of his desk holding his chest. Oh my God! Was he having a heart attack? Before she could unfreeze herself to run to him, red began to seep from under his hand. That's no heart attack. Slowly, without thinking, she swung the door open further. She tensed, realizing that she was a few feet away from two men in expensive looking suits.

One was tall, with a frame like a bodybuilder. He had dark hair and tattoos covering a neck she thought would be as thick as her head. A gun hung loosely in his right hand.

The other guy was standing closer to her. He was of average height for a man, his head covered in an old-fashioned fedora. He turned to look at her. There was intelligence and malice in his dark eyes. *Shit.*

"I told you to lock the fucking door, Booker," the man in the fedora muttered.

"Sorry, Boss."

The boss scowled at her. "Ms. Robertson, it seems we have a problem."

Sloane didn't wait a moment longer; she turned and ran. No way was she waiting for the elevator either. She barreled through the door that lead to the stairs. A floor down, she heard a door open above. Was it the same floor she'd just exited? *Shit. Shit. Shit.* Her damn heels gave her position away easily. Hopping on one foot, then the other, she removed her shoes without stopping her quick decent. She should enter one of the other floors and take the elevator, but what if the other man was waiting inside the car? No, this way was safer.

A metallic ping! sounded off the railing where her hand had just been, sending sparks flying off. The big brute was shooting at her! Safer, her ass. Without her shoes she could jump down the last few steps on each floor. After what seemed like hours, she plowed into the door full force, finally entering the crowded lobby.

The moment the door opened, everything crawled by in slow motion; each step felt as if she was running underwater. He had to be gaining on her at this speed. Looking behind her for the brute called Booker, she ran right into a hard flesh wall. Panic had her throwing herself backward away from the arms grabbing her shoulders. This was it. The killer had her. She was going to die, all because she was dedicated to her job. Squeezing her eyes closed, she braced herself for the inevitable gunshot that still hadn't come.

"Sloane?"

She knew that voice. That voice had haunted her dreams the past two nights. Slowly, she opened her eyes. Max stood next to the man who held her arms, keeping her from fleeing. The man in front of her looked to be in his early forties.

The man took a step back, and Max took her into his arms and tucked her head under his chin. "What happened?" Max asked. "Are you okay?"

"M-M-Mr. Marek…"

"What about him. Did he do something to you?" Anger laced each word.

"Shot. Upstairs."

"Lock this place down!" the other man yelled at the security desk. "NOW."

***

Max

Max led Sloane over to one of the couches in the airy lobby. She was white as a ghost and shaking uncontrollably. He sat down next to her and pulled her toward him, tucking her under his arm. It was not the time to think of how perfectly she fit there.

How perfect she felt.

Winston made his way over to them after speaking with the building's security. He knelt down in front of her, taking one of her hands in his.

"Ms. Robertson, my name is Winston Peters."

"Y-you...you were Mr. Marek's two o'clock."

"I was. Now tell me everything you saw."

Sloane gulped. "I was rushing back to get prepared for your meeting. I...I entered Mr. Marek's office to hang his dry cleaning in his closet. I never heard a gunshot, but I s-s-saw...saw the blood appear on his shirt. Two men in suits were there. The one in charge called the other one, 'Booker.' I ran down the stairs. Booker followed, and he...he *s-shot* at me. Then I ran into you."

"Did they say anything else to you? Think, it's important."

"Just before I ran, the short one said, 'Ms. Robertson, it seems we have a problem.'"

"He used your name?"

"Yes."

"Are you certain?"

"Yes, I'm sure of it."

Max met Winston's eyes over Sloane's head. This wasn't good. No way could she go back to her apartment with the killers knowing her name. She might not know both of their names, but she knew their faces. Max continued to rub circles across her back to calm her. Eventually, uniformed officers came to get her statement.

"Sloane, Winston and I are going over there to speak with the detective. Give this officer the best descriptions you can, but don't leave without me.

Understand?"

"Sure," she mumbled.

"Sloane, do you understand?" he demanded.

"I understand."

He hated walking away from her. She seemed so lost and vulnerable as she stared at the marble floor. He stalked to where Winston stood waiting; he wanted to get this over with and get back to Sloane. Today was not going the way he'd planned. He'd thought he would use today's meeting to see her. Maybe even get the courage to ask her to dinner. He could even spin it as a wedding thing since she was the maid of honor. Tell her that since he was the best man, they should work together to surprise the happy couple with something. That idea was shot to hell now.

"She's in danger," Winston said.

"I know. Shit."

"How do you know her? Ex?"

"No, she's the cousin of Foster's fiancée. We met the other night at dinner."

"I didn't see a ring. Any other family at home that we need to get to?"

"No, a boyfriend, but they don't live together. He's a cop. How are you holding up? I know you guys went way back."

"Detlef should have called me sooner, damn it. He never listened to me."

Max patted Winston's shoulder as Sloane stood up. She scanned the lobby until her eyes settled on him. He met her halfway, taking her face into his hands. As he skimmed his thumbs across her cheekbones, she inhaled a ragged breath.

"Are you sure you're okay?"

"As okay as I can be. I should call Brody. I can't be alone tonight."

Brody. How stupid could Max be? Of *course* she would want to be with her boyfriend. He was a cop, so he was perfectly capable of protecting her. Why Max had entertained the notion that she would want him to take care of her, he had no fucking idea. Against his better judgment, Max put his arm around her shoulders.

"Let's go outside. You can call him out there."

"Thank you, Max. You helped keep me sane in there. I don't know what I would have done had you not been here."

Max stood next to her as she called Brody. Three times it went to voicemail. She sighed. The sound spoke of disappointment. He wanted to kiss her again and make her see she was wasting her time on a man who couldn't appreciate her. He was just about to do that very thing, when she lifted the phone and dialed yet again.

"Hey, I'm sorry to bother you."

Max listened to the one-sided conversation. It definitely wasn't Brody.

"...Sounds like fun. I hate to ask, but what time was Brody on tonight?...Oh. Okay...I see...No. No, that's all right...I'll come by tomorrow...Love you guys too."

After a minute of pleasantries, Max realized Foster was on the other end of the phone.

Sloane ended the call, slumping against the side of the building. He stood beside her silently for a few moments. Finally, he slid his finger under her chin, tipping her head up to look at him. Max felt like he had been sucker punched—the resigned defeat in her eyes crushed something deep inside him.

"What happened? Does Foster know where Brody is?"

Tears glistened in her eyes. She tried to blink them back, but one spilled slowly down her cheek. He swiped it away with the pad of his thumb.

"He doesn't know. His shift ended over an hour ago."

"You're coming home with me."

"What? I can't do that."

"Why not?"

He watched the expressions fly across her face as she tried to come up with an answer. "Because…well, because."

"I'm not asking you to jump in bed with me. Although, I would be a damn moron to refuse if you wanted to."

He winked at her, hoping his humor would lighten up the situation some. Her eyes widened in shock. The look was innocent and damn near undid him.

"I have a spare room. You can stay there as long as you want. You shouldn't be alone and honestly, it may not be safe at your apartment."

"I didn't think of that," she said, her voice barely a whisper. "Thank you, Max."

"Don't mention it."

Chapter Six

Sloane

Sloane followed Max back to his house, constantly watching the mirrors trying to see if she was being followed like in the crime dramas she loved to watch. It only took a few minutes for her to admit that she didn't know what the hell she was doing. At least she didn't have to go back to her apartment alone tonight.

The city slowly fell away, leaving open fields and small farms before her. The smell of manure was strong, but surprisingly not as repulsive as one would think. Caught up in the simple beauty surrounding her, she almost missed Max turning down a hidden gravel driveway.

The two-story, brick-colored farmhouse coming into view was quaint. The white wraparound porch was inviting to friends and strangers alike. Black shutters framed each window.

Momentary jealousy niggled its way in. It looked like the dream house she had pictured in her head since she was a child. She couldn't wait to see inside. She continued on the gravel driveway as it curved behind the house and parked in the small lot beside Max.

He stood at the bottom of the steps, hands stuffed in his front pockets, waiting. He appeared almost shy the way he looked everywhere except at her. He led her inside after unlocking the heavy wood door, his hand warm on the small of her back. Simplistic and homey, the kitchen was uncluttered, but definitely lived in.

Lemon chiffon curtains brightened up the room. White hand towels with little yellow flowers had Sloane wondering who decorated. What if Max didn't live alone? Would a suspicious girlfriend make more out of this than there was? Maybe this wasn't such a good idea.

"Will your girlfriend be upset that I'm here? I don't want to cause any problems."

"Is that your way of asking if I'm available?"

The grin he flashed over his shoulder was panty melting. Holy smokes, Max was sexy. *No.* Sloane needed to stay focused. Not salivating over the perfection that was his ass. Still she followed him around his house like a puppy.

"Um…No. I just didn't want her to be upset that I'm here."

Max stopped suddenly. Whirling around, he crowded her personal space. His cologne was subtle—spicy and tempting like the man wearing it. His eyes were blazing. She could feel the heat between her thighs. She swallowed hard.

"If I was living with another woman, do you

really think I would have kissed you after dinner the other night?"

She stepped back. "I don't know. I don't really know you, now do I?"

She certainly wasn't living with Brody, but he sure as hell had done more than just kiss other girls since they had been together. Something resembling hurt flashed over Max's face, but it flitted away quickly before fortitude and anger took its place. Max could go from sexy to scary in a heartbeat. She refused to admit both turned her on.

"When I'm involved with a woman, Sloane, I'm with her and only her. I know you don't have much experience with men who respect monogamy, but *I* do."

Standing up straighter, she glared at him. "Hey! My relationship is none of your damn business. Who the hell do you think you are?"

"I'm the man you can count on tonight."

His words hurt as they were meant to. Sloane held back the tears that were threatening to spill. No way would she give him the satisfaction of seeing he got to her.

"Follow me, I'll show you to your room."

His tone was clipped, cold even. She didn't respond; there was nothing to say.

She followed him up the stairs to the second floor. The wall going up was covered in photographs. Some were decades old, others just a few years. They looked like they spanned generations. One of Max in his police blues struck such a strong emotion in her, she almost tripped up the steps. That would've been smooth. Shaking her head, she continued the climb.

The room Max stopped in front of was immaculate. The bed was covered in floral bedspread that matched the sheer curtains. The dresser and bed frame looked like expensive cherry wood, not that cheap pressed wood that was so popular these days. Like the other rooms she had seen, this one also sported hardwood floors with plush carpet runners protecting the varnish in high-traffic areas. It was stunning.

"You can stay in here."

"It's beautiful."

He kept talking like she hadn't said anything at all. "The bathroom is the next room on the right. On the left is my room should you need anything. I'll get you something to sleep in. We can get some of your things tomorrow."

He left her still standing in the doorway as he stalked off to his room. He came back a few moments later with a pair of sweatpants, a large t-shirt, and an unopened toothbrush. They were barely in her hands before he was walking away, back down the steps.

She called out to him. "Thank you, Max."

"Couldn't let you go home alone. It wouldn't be right."

Sloane watched until Max disappeared from sight before closing herself in the unfamiliar room. Sadness and loneliness closed in around her. Curling up on the soft mattress, she felt the dam open inside of her. Tears flowed freely. Soft sobs wracked her body. It could have been minutes or hours before sleep finally rescued her from her melancholy.

***

Max

Twenty minutes had passed and still no Sloane. Max had thought she would've been right behind him once she put the clothes he gave her into her room. Maybe he'd been too hard on her.

Thinking he should check on her, he hiked back upstairs and stopped just outside the closed door. Leaning in to listen, he could faintly make out the weeping inside. *Shit.* Why did he have to be such an ass earlier? Sure, she had insulted him, insinuating that he was just another cheating bastard. Did she think so little of him? Or did she think so little of all men? Foster certainly didn't seem to bear the brunt of any ill will.

Placing his hand on the door, he thought about knocking. He should apologize, but he couldn't. He couldn't bear to face the hurt he had caused. Not while both of their feelings were still so raw. Slowly, his hand slid down the door in defeat.

He made his way back downstairs to the kitchen to make a sandwich for himself. He would make Sloane one if and when she came out of her room later. Plopped in front of his television, Max scanned through the channels while he ate his turkey sandwich. By the time he finished eating, there still wasn't anything on that he cared to watch. He pulled his cell phone from his pocket and brought up the contact information for Foster.

"Hey man, what's up?"

"You talked to Sloane earlier, so you have the majority of it."

"Yeah, she puts on a good face, but she seemed a little trampled on."

"She was."

Max recounted the events of the day as he'd remembered her describing to him. He pictured her face as she bolted out of the stairwell, right into Winston's arms. He'd wished it was his arms she ran into. She'd felt so good pressed up against him as she waited to give her statement.

Foster's voice brought him out of his haze.

"She must have been terrified."

"All she wanted was that sorry excuse of a boyfriend to comfort her."

"I made some calls after I talked to her. Brody told one of his buddies he was going to see Carmela after his shift. I'll give Sloane a call to see how she's holding up."

"She's upset, but all right. She's lying down."

"How would you know?"

"They knew her name, Foster. Probably her address as well. No way could she go back there, much less go there alone."

"She never told me that earlier. This isn't good."

"My sentiments exactly."

"All right, I'll try to work around mine and Bella's schedule so she isn't ever alone. I know your rule about women, but can she stay there tonight? Or should I come get her?"

"No, she's fine. You don't have to rearrange anything. I don't have anything I need to do for a few days that require me to leave the house. She can stay here."

"You really are sweet on her, aren't you?"

"Shut up, dude. I'm just trying to help her out."

"You keep telling yourself that. Maybe you'll even start believing it. All right, man, take care of her. I'll touch base with you tomorrow."

Max slumped back against the couch after disconnecting the call, scrubbing his face with his hands. The burdens of the day settled unacceptably on his shoulders. Resigned that there was nothing more he could do tonight, he made his way up to bed, stopping first to brush his teeth. The toothbrush he had giving Sloane was open on the countertop.

He stopped by her door again. All was silent inside. Opening it quietly, Max peered inside to make sure she was okay.

Sloane was wrapped around one of the many pillows that covered the bed, her long porcelain legs cradling part of the cushion. Her golden hair spilled over another. She had changed into nothing more than the shirt he had supplied, and it had ridden up, just barely hiding the swell of her ass cheeks. Her soft moan brought his dick to attention. Silently, he backed out of the room and marched to his own. How the hell was he supposed to sleep now?

Tossing and turning, Max couldn't get the image of Sloane spread across the bed in the next room out of his mind. The way the moonlight illuminated her skin, causing it to practically glow. What would it feel like to touch her? To run his hands over her velvety skin? Grasping his shaft, he began stroking it slowly, imagining Sloane's supple thighs wrapped around him.

His strokes became longer, pulling harder as his hips thrust up involuntarily to meet his hand. Max pictured her above him. Her golden tresses falling across his chest. Slowly his orgasm built, quickening his breath. He was close. A few more thrusts and he would find sweet release. Knowing Sloane was in the next room just made it hotter.

Her sudden scream of "Max!" brought his orgasm instantly. Only his concern kept him from truly enjoying the moment. He donned his boxer briefs after using a towel to clean off the evidence from his stomach, even as he left the privacy of his bedroom. Without knocking, he entered the room. Sloane was sitting on the bed with her knees up to her chin, her arms wrapped tightly around them. She looked terrified. Max rushed to her side, lowering himself onto the mattress next to her. He pulled her head against his chest.

"It's okay, babe, I'm here. Everything is all right."

"I was being chased. He almost had me this time."

"It was just a dream."

"I'm so sorry, Max. I didn't mean to wake you. I feel ridiculous."

"I wasn't asleep. No reason for apologies. You're safe here. I'll never let anyone hurt you."

"Will you…will you stay here with me?" She focused on her hands, which were absently rubbing the tops of her feet. She quickly added, "Just until I fall back asleep?"

***

Sloane

Sloane felt stupid and vulnerable after Max darted into her temporary room. She was hugging herself, trying to chase Booker's face from her memory. Every time she closed her eyes, his face appeared. She could imagine him chasing her through the stairwell. Max didn't seem to mind, though. He pulled her close, rubbing her arm to comfort her.

Even when she asked him to stay, he didn't berate her or make excuses why he couldn't. He leaned back onto the headboard, bringing her along with him. She slipped her arms around his waist and snuggled her head against his shoulder. She felt safe with him. The steady rhythm of his breathing soothed her to sleep quickly.

Chapter Seven

Sloane

Tightening her arms around Brody, Sloane sighed. Her elbow brushed against his growing erection. Unable to help herself, she moaned, rubbing her cheek against his bare chest slowly. Her leg was thrown over his, leaving his thigh pressed against her core. Could he feel the heat through her panties? It had been over a month since they'd had sex.

Feeling brave for the first time in her life, she cupped his balls and then slid her hand up his shaft. The dull throb between her legs had her grinding herself against him slowly as his cock continued to lengthen in her hand.

"Now *this* could persuade me to like mornings."

Giggling, she opened her eyes to look up at Brody's face. Only it wasn't Brody—it was Max looking down at her, a mixture of surprise, confusion, and desire storming in his eyes. They were breathtaking. Sloane's brain finally came

59

online. She remembered the events that led to her being in bed with Max.

"Ohmygod!" Sloane jumped up and stumbled halfway across the room, her hand covering her open mouth...until she realized it was the same hand that had just caressed Max's dick. She quickly dropped it to her side. She could feel the flames dancing across her skin. With her pale complexion, she knew without a doubt her entire face and neck must resemble a beet. She was incredibly mortified.

"I am so sorry, Max!" she squeaked.

He laughed, standing up from the bed in nothing but a pair of black boxer briefs that were more than slightly raised in the front. "It's okay."

He tried to adjust himself inconspicuously, but seeing as she couldn't take her eyes off of him, he really didn't need to bother. His tanned chest was expansive, and lightly dusted with dark hair that covered his pecks and trailed down his mouthwatering abs to end somewhere past the elastic of his briefs. Tattoos swirled around his biceps in no discernible pattern. Sloane longed to trace each one with her fingertips...and her tongue.

He had the thickest thighs she'd ever seen on a man. At least on someone who wasn't a professional bodybuilder. They screamed of power. What would those muscles feel like contracting underneath her? How could she have mistaken his body for Brody's? Brody was a puny awkward teenage boy compared to Max.

"I can't believe I just molested you like that. I'm truly horrified." She covered her face with her hands, though she peeked between her fingers to gauge his reaction.

Max stalked across the room like a prowling panther and grabbed her shoulders. She dropped her hands by her side. His whiskey-colored eyes penetrated hers, holding her mesmerized and silent in their depths. She swallowed hard, having no choice but to give him her undivided attention.

"First off, stop apologizing. Secondly, I could have easily moved your hand at any time. Thirdly, it should be *me* apologizing."

"You? For what?"

"I should have realized you didn't know it was me. You wouldn't have done that if you did. I should have stopped you, but I didn't."

He took a step back, dropping his hands. She would have wanted to, though. Even standing here like a statue, she wanted to reach for him. The loss of heat on her skin from his hands almost pulled a whimper from inside her. The awareness she felt with Max was staggering.

There had never been a time before now where she'd felt every nerve come alive inside of her from just the touch of someone's hand. When he'd smiled, it made her insides melt.

"I'm gonna go get dressed. Then I'll make some breakfast. You must be starving."

"Um, sure. I could eat."

Sloane watched his chiseled ass as he made his retreat from the room. She was still in shock at what she did. She'd never initiated things with Brody. What made her try this time? Did her subconscious know it was Max all along? Dropping down onto the mattress, she replayed the incident in her head.

Her body craved him. She'd mourned the loss of his warm flesh pressed against hers. Damn, she had to get herself in check. Dressing in yesterday's clothes, she left the sanctity of the bedroom, mentally preparing herself to see Max again.

The smell of cooking bacon had her practically salivating. When was the last time she ate? Max stood over the burners, flipping bacon and scrambling eggs. He was covered by a thin white ribbed tank top that clung to every muscle and a pair of worn blue jeans. He was barefoot and the top button of his pants was still undone. The heat that rushed through her had her clamping her thighs together. Too bad it only made matters worse. Max was incredibly sexy.

"Good timing."

He piled food onto a plate. After setting it in front of her, he took the seat beside her with his own plate. They ate in companionable silence, until finally she looked over at him as he read the paper.

"So what now?"

"Now we sit tight and wait."

"Wait for what, exactly?"

"For me to get some reliable intel so we can find this guy. Until then, you'll stay here with me. I can keep you safe."

"What about your job?"

"I can do everything I need to for my current workload from the comfort of my home office. So don't worry. Okay?"

"Okay," she sighed.

"What, no argument?"

"You're right. No sense arguing."

Sloane finished her breakfast quietly. She cleared their dishes from the table. She was startled when the wall phone rang by her head.

Max pushed to his feet and walked over to grab it. "Hello."

There was a long pause before Max turned, his body stiffening slightly. He handed his phone out toward her. Sloane took it, a questioning look no doubt on her face. Max looked less than happy.

"It's for you."

For her? Foster and Bella must be wondering what in the world was going on. Maybe she could stay with them for a few days instead. She took the phone from Max's outstretched hand.

"Hello?"

"Sloane, honey, are you okay?" Brody's voice boomed through the handset.

"I'm fine. How did you know I was here?"

"I called Foster. He reamed me out pretty good after he told me what happened."

She looked at Max. He casually leaned against the doorframe, his arms crossed in front of him. He was so damn striking that it was harder than she would have thought to pay attention to the conversation she was having. Watching him was too distracting. Mentally, she took a deep breath, fortifying her resolve to not even think about falling for a man like him. It would only lead to heartache and she'd had enough of that in her life. Her gaze fixed on anything other than the handsome man in the room with her. See, look how interesting the stove was.

"Where were you?"

"I was home, honey. My phone died so I had it charging. I'll be more careful in the future."

"Your phone was dead all night?"

Sloane could feel the pinpricks of tears forming in her eyes. Even though she had no real way of knowing for sure, deep down she knew Brody was lying. She risked a glance up at Max. The anger coming off of him was almost visible. Could he hear Brody on the other end of the line? She must look like a damn fool. Everyone at the station knew about Brody's indiscretions. They were the perfect alibi for him. All except Foster. He was like Big Brother, always watching out for her, even when she didn't want him to.

"Of course not, but I went to sleep while it was still charging. I'm sorry, honey. Do you want me to come get you? I can drop you at your apartment before I go to the station."

"No, I'll be fine."

"With Max?"

Brody's loving boyfriend façade started to slip. There was an underlying hostility in his voice, and it grew stronger with each word he spoke. It almost sounded like jealousy, which was ridiculous—he had never been the jealous type in the past. Then again, she had never given him a reason to be.

"Are you fucking him, Sloane?"

"No. My God, how can you even think that? I'm not like you, Brody. I don't fuck everything with a dick just because I can."

"Most men would get frostbite after one night with you. You're lucky I stick around like I do."

Sloane gasped, covering her mouth with her free

hand, the other squeezing the phone like a lifeline. She was temporarily unable to process the meaning behind his words. She couldn't believe he'd just said that. The tears she fought so hard to hold back came streaming down her cheeks with a vengeance.

Max pushed away from the wall and stalked toward her. She held up a hand in a stop motion. No way could she let him interfere—she had to get used to doing things on her own again. She had to be the one to do this. She had to break this cycle, but Brody kept right on talking.

"I looked at you and thought I'd won the lotto. I was wrong. How can a woman as hot as you be so fucking dead inside?"

Every word was like a knife through her heart. She cared about him...*no*. Maybe what she really cared about now was the person he had been, but he hadn't been *that* Brody in some time. The sex wasn't great now like it had been in the past. That was before Brody thought their sex life should resemble a BDSM porn flick. Not that she thought there was anything wrong with them, but that life just wasn't for her. She'd thought that as long as there was open communication, two people in love could work that out.

She wasn't really in love with him yet, but there had been potential. If he only could've kept his dick in his pants.

But no more. Now, she was through bending over backwards to try to please him.

"You're right. I'm sorry. I tried. I really did try to be what you wanted, but obviously I failed. This isn't working."

"What are you talking about?"

"This, us. It's over. I can't do it anymore."

Sloane hung up the phone before Brody could say anything else. Her face was damp with spilled tears. She couldn't stand the idea of Max witnessing another meltdown, so she pushed past him. She didn't stop moving until she was curled up on the bed again.

She did it. She'd ended things with Brody. How could she have been so stupid? For almost a year she stayed with him knowing deep down it was wrong. She should have walked after the first time she caught him with another woman. Not that any of it mattered anymore. Sloane lay there for a long time. Long after her sobs ceased. Today would hurt. She would let the pain wash over her. She would feel everything and let it be a reminder to her future self. Today would hurt, but tomorrow she would be better.

***

Max

Max was beyond furious. He wanted to put his fist through that asshole's face. Thinking of Sloane upstairs crying only made it worse. He wanted to go to her. Wrap her in his arms and tell her it was the best thing she could have done, but he knew she wouldn't let him. As much as he wanted to, he knew he shouldn't. He couldn't let himself get more attached than he already was. He didn't do relationships, and even if he did, he wasn't good enough for someone like her. He would only hurt her in the end, and she was already broken enough. That's what he kept telling himself.

Needing to release some of the pent-up aggression, Max opened the door to the basement and descended into his personal gym. The room wasn't huge, but it was all he needed. An exercise bike sat along the wall, across from the clothes washer and dryer. Next to that, a treadmill. The adjacent wall framed in the weight bench and the shelving for all the free weights. A punching bag and medicine bag rounded out the equipment before him. He clicked on the radio already tuned to a station that played a little bit of everything. This is what he needed to keep his head straight.

He unbuttoned his jeans and pulled them off, replacing them with a pair of athletic shorts he hadn't yet removed from the dryer. His running shoes were where he'd left them by the weight bench. After slipping them on, he positioned himself on the side rails of the treadmill.

Max set the pace slow to warm up, and his feet touched the conveyer belt in a slow jog. After a few minutes his thoughts quieted completely. Nothing except his breathing and the music on his mind. Max could feel the tension draining slowly from his body. The DJ stopped talking and a song about a woman being out of the singer's league poured from the surround sound speakers. Instantly he thought of Sloane.

Yup. That about sums it up in a nutshell. Knowing that didn't stop his thoughts from returning to this morning. The way she'd held onto him, sliding her silky leg up his rough one. Did she register the sharp intake of his breath when she wrapped her hand around his balls, sliding up his shaft? No matter how hard he'd tried, he couldn't keep his body from responding. A few more minutes of that, and he would've had her on her back spread before him. It was like a dream, a sexy fantasy about to be fulfilled. Until she raised those gorgeous baby blues to his.

The fantasy shattered into a million pieces as embarrassment washed across her features. Even that was adorable as all hell. After fisting himself to completion last night thinking of those perfect legs, it was nice to know she was just as affected by him as he was by her. It was the regret and realization that he wasn't Brody that ruined it. He'd kept things light, acting as if it were no big deal. But inside, he'd been berating himself.

He couldn't think of her like that anymore. He needed to put her in a mental box. Label her, "client," and maybe his dick would stop trying to do his thinking for him. He never crossed the line with his clients. Maybe that was the answer to this whole clusterfuck.

A loud rock song came on next. It was one that he couldn't remember the name to, but it helped set his resolve. Kicking up the speed, Max started running. Focusing on the beat, he let the music take him away. Sweat ran down the sides of his face, stinging his eyes.

Occasionally he dabbed his face on a towel that hung over the handrail of the machine. His shirt was soaked through, clinging to him everywhere. He wasn't sure how long he ran. The burn in his muscles indicated it was a long time.

He slowed the machine down. He walked long enough to avoid cramping before he pulled the tank top off and threw it into the almost empty hamper.

Retrieving a bottle of water, he cracked the seal and had drunk half of it by the time he reached the living room. The light on his answering machine blinked rapidly, informing him there was a message waiting. He pressed Play, finishing off his water while listening.

"Maxwell, honey, it's mom. I'm sorry I missed you again. I worry about you; give me a call. I love you."

Beep.

"Heeeyyyy, Max. It's Charlie. I haven't heard from you in a while, baby. I was hoping you'd come over to play. Get your handcuffs ready and call me back."

Beep.

Max shook his head, a small smile lifting one side of his mouth. Charlie was one of his "go-to girls." She didn't mind a casual thing. That was perfect for Max. He didn't want anything permanent.

Right now, though, what he needed was a shower to wash the sweat drying on his skin away. As he stood up, he saw Sloane standing on the bottom of the steps watching him. Her hair was ruffled and her cheek had creases from the pillow. She was adorable.

He had made up his mind—this woman was not going to get to him. He wasn't desperate. He could have Charlie purring around him with a simple phone call. Maybe that's what he needed. Someone to take the edge off. It'd been a couple of months since he'd had anything more than a self-service release. It was about time he had something other than his own hand. After he showered, he would give her a call. Mind made up, he leisurely walked toward the steps.

***

Sloane

"Heeeyyyy, Max. It's Charlie. I haven't heard from you in a while, baby. I was hoping you'd come over to play. Get your handcuffs ready and call me back."

The message kept playing on a loop in Sloane's head. She stood motionless, watching Max grin at the machine. When their eyes locked, his still held desire, but in an instant it was gone. They were just eyes, not the heated amber orbs that had held her captive since they'd met. Pain radiated in her chest; she had to stop herself from physically rubbing it.

Max walked toward her slowly. In nothing except running shorts, his golden brown body glistened with sweat. She wanted to trace his dark nipples with her tongue, making them peak for her pleasure and her pleasure alone. Everything about him was massive, and she wanted to own it all…No, she wanted him to own *her*.

"I'm gonna grab a shower. Then we can head over to Foster's to fill them in." He looked like the same Max, but his voice was different—distant, professional. His body was stiff and his eyes lacked anything more than cool detachment. "After that, we'll pick up some of your things. How are you holding up?"

Her tongue felt like it was glued to the roof of her mouth as she pictured water running over intimate parts of his body. Blinking a few times, she focused on the step below her.

"I'm fine. I'll be fine. No need to worry."

"I won't be long. Give me ten minutes."

Max left her standing there, taking two steps at a time up the stairs. Maybe she had misread the signals he'd been sending earlier? No, no way. They were clear as day. Plus, that kiss was proof positive of something happening between them. Maybe he'd heard Brody earlier and changed his mind. A man like him, or any man for that matter, wouldn't want to get involved with a woman described as cold or dead inside.

She didn't feel like that at all with Max. She felt the electricity all around her when he was near. Her blood boiled. Butterflies took up residence in her stomach when he looked at her...at least they had until this last time. This time she was filled with dread and longing.

"I was hoping you'd come over to play. Get your handcuffs ready and call me back."

The words haunted Sloane. The sweet silkiness of the woman's voice made it all too easy to picture the type of woman who got to experience the irresistibleness that was Max. Sloane bet she was tall with legs that never ended. She sounded like the type to have a piercing in her taut belly—not to mention other places. Without an inch of fat, she probably oozed sex with every move she made. Sloane instantly hated her.

She ran back upstairs and retrieved her cell phone from her purse. It showed fifteen missed calls. Two from her parents' house. One from Mirabella. The remaining twelve from Brody. All time stamped after their talk earlier. Yup, not going there. She shot Bella a text letting her know that they would be there shortly, then put her phone away. She'd call her parents later.

Max stepped out of the bathroom with a towel secured around his waist. The vision of him was breathtaking. She wanted to pull the offending cotton off and beg him to bend her over the rail—*Whoa.* She was really starting to lose it. He glanced at her out of the corner of his eye, but never said anything as he continued down the small hallway, shutting the door behind him once he was inside his bedroom. She hurried down the steps. She didn't stop until she was on the back porch trying to catch her breath. She was in trouble. Given half a chance, that man could break her heart.

Chapter Eight

Sloane

They drove in silence to Bella's house. Only the road noise and the sound of his keypad typing multiple text messages filled the cabin of the truck. Who kept the sound of their keyboard on, anyway? Sloane watched the fields go by out of the passenger window. After observing him grin at his phone a few minutes ago, she couldn't bear to look at him anymore. The betrayal she felt didn't make any damn sense. Until just a few short hours ago she'd had a boyfriend. A shitty, lying, cheating boyfriend, but a boyfriend just the same.

She and Max had never been an item. Sure, he'd kissed her once. Now she could almost admit to herself how much she'd liked it. She shouldn't feel anything for this man, though. She knew he wasn't the type to stick around. That didn't stop her from wanting him anyway.

She needed a night out. A reason to get dressed up and dance away whatever was making her pine for the man sitting next to her.

Once they were parked—in what she was starting to think of as Max's spot—she practically jumped from the truck. She briskly marched up the steps and let herself inside without waiting for Max to catch up. He knew where the door was. The less time she spent with him, the better.

"Bella," Sloane yelled once she was inside.

"Hey. I'm upstairs."

Taking the steps two at a time, she found Bella putting away a basket of laundry. Once again she was in a dress, baby blue with little white flowers and her hair pulled back. Only this time her outfit was paired with a simple pair of flats. They resembled the old ballet slippers Sloane had when she was a kid.

Sloane was a jeans and t-shirt kind of a girl most days. She enjoyed dressing up, but only when there was an occasion to do so.

"Hey, honey."

Bella embraced her, hugging her harder than she expected. Given everything she had experienced in the last twenty-four hours, she admitted she needed it more than she would have thought.

Sloane sobbed into her cousin's neck. "I did it."

"Did what? Oh my…did you sleep with Max?" She said the last part in a shriek as she pulled back, her impish smile willing Sloane to give her a clue. Any clue as to whether or not she had a salacious sexual encounter with one Max Fear.

"Why does everyone think I'm doing Max?"

"Because he's seriously hot and I see the way he looks at you. Wait, what…everyone? Who else thinks you're banging Max?" She frowned, her eyebrows pinching together.

"Brody accused me of it just before I ended things with him."

"Thank you sweet baby Jesus!" Bella pumped her fist in the air before twirling around in circles doing her happy dance.

The scene brought on a burst of laughter from Sloane. The last time she had seen Bella this happy was when Foster proposed. Her laughter was contagious. Sloane couldn't not join in when it was this sincere. But like a switch that had been flipped, Bella's face took on a solemn expression and she fixed her gaze on Sloane.

"Oh, honey, I'm sorry. I didn't even ask how you're taking this."

"I need to go out. Like, tonight. I wanna get dressed up and paint the town. I need to forget all about him. Even if it's only for a few hours with a good lookin' stranger."

"Now you're talkin', sister." She craned her neck and raised her voice. "Hey, Foster!"

Mirabella yelled loud enough to make Sloane wince and wonder if she'd ever regain all her hearing in her right ear. She was rubbing her sore ear when Foster, followed by Max, came strolling in the bedroom. At least Max wasn't wearing that sexy smile while gazing at his phone anymore.

"You called, my dear?" Foster kissed Bella's cheek and slipped his arm around her.

"Yes. Sloane and I are going out tonight. I just wanted you to know." She moved out from under Foster's embrace. She stood next to Sloane, looping her arm over Sloane's shoulder in a show of sisterly solidarity. Her smile bright as could be.

"Tonight?"

"Yup, she got rid of Mr. Wrong and tonight she's gonna find Mr. Right Now."

"Not a good idea," Max piped in immediately. Sloane wanted to punch him in the mouth.

"And why not?" She put her fists on her hips. Who did he think he was? Her father?

"Because it might not be safe," he answered smugly. Well the hell with that.

"Hey, Foster, why don't you call some of your friends and we can go as a group. I'll be safe as can be among all of you lawmen." Sloane winked at him and gave him what she hoped was her best smile.

"Actually, that sounds pretty cool. I'll send a mass text message. What time?"

"The Void at eight sharp."

Bella grabbed both of Sloane's hands, once again twirling in her happy dance after Foster confirmed his message was sent. Max looked like he'd just finished sucking on a lemon. Where was that seductive little smile now? Ha! The men went back to whatever it was they'd been doing downstairs as the girls discussed important things like hair and makeup.

***

Max

Well shit, Max thought, trailing Foster back

downstairs. He had already made plans to see Charlie tonight to relieve a little stress. Maybe Foster wouldn't mind dropping Sloane off at his place afterward for him. Even after thinking it, it sounded like a shitty thing to ask. Since he wasn't sure what time he would be back there.

"Nice, Mother and Tank are in," Foster called behind him.

"Cool. So, dude, I kinda had a date tonight." Max squirmed, waiting for a reaction.

"Really? I'd assumed—I thought—you had a thing for Sloane? She's single now. Did you miss that part?"

"She's great, but we both know I'm not one to settle down yet." Although the more Max said it, the less he believed it.

Foster shrugged. "It's your life. Since you appointed yourself as her unofficial bodyguard, I'd thought that you would be with her at all times." Foster took a seat on the couch. "Oh, well…that's all right. She wouldn't want to be a burden to you. Anyway, between me, Mother, and Tank, she'll be fine. Sloane can stay here tonight. You know…if she needs a place."

Foster checked his phone again while Max thought of what "if she needs a place" could mean. Max ignored the blatant accusation of him leaving Sloane alone since Foster had been the one adamantly against it in the first place…Wait, Foster didn't think she'd let a strange man take her home tonight, did he? That's sure as hell what it'd sounded like. The thought left a bad taste in Max's mouth.

"Now it's a party. Gutter Mouth is a go. I repeat, Gutter Mouth is a go." Foster laughed.

Oh hell no. He couldn't leave Sloane alone with Gutter Mouth. The man was a stand-up guy, but a hound when it came to women. Sloane was just his type: soft, sweet, and curves in all the right places. Maybe he could bring Charlie to the club? Kill two birds with one stone. Yeah, that could work. Watch Sloane at the club and have Charlie afterward. Perfect.

When Sloane was ready to go, they got in his truck. The next stop was to her place for clothes and whatever else women needed to get through each day. There was a heaviness in the air Max was afraid to disturb. He parked out front of the building, and they walked in together. It was a very different journey from the last time he walked her to her door. He certainly wouldn't be tasting her sweet lips again.

The elevator ride was made in silence. Max noticed for the first time that she hadn't actually looked him in the eye since he walked passed her to take a shower that morning. It bothered him. Things were better off this way, he reasoned with himself.

Everything else seemed normal—that is, until they got to her apartment. Someone had certainly been there. Furniture had been overturned, glass littered the floor, and picture frames had been shattered.

Max held his hand up, stopping her from passing the threshold. "Let me go first. Wait out here until I call you."

"But—"

"Just do it, damn it," Max barked. "This is my job." He was harsher than he'd meant to be, but her safety was what mattered most at this moment, not her feelings.

Max entered the apartment without waiting for another protest. He pulled a small Kahr PM9 from his waistband at the small of his back. There was no way to tell if the house was clear. Other than surface damage, there wasn't a whole lot to clean up. Jewelry was still inside the velvet box on her dresser and all the electronics were still in place, so robbery was most likely not a motivator. It was a message. They knew where she lived. Making his way from room to room, Max checked every nook of her apartment before he let her inside.

"Clear, you can come in now." He tucked his weapon back in his waistband.

She murmured so softly Max barely heard her, "Shit."

"Get what you need for a few days. You can't come back here until we find these guys. We need to call the police too."

"Okay."

Max studied Sloane as she pulled out her cell phone. She explained the situation quickly before hanging up. Tears welled up in her eyes. After a brief moment, she looked at him. Really looked at him. Startled, she sniffed the tears back, straightening her shoulders. That haunted expression had him wanting to drop to his knees in front of her. Promise her the world just to see her smile again.

It took over three hours to finish up with the

police. In all that time, she barely glanced his way. Max passed some of the time talking to Detective Owen Chance. They went to the academy together a lifetime ago. Max didn't miss being on the force, but he did miss a few of the guys he'd once worked with. Once everyone was gone, Sloane was free to retrieve her things. She came out twenty minutes later with a small suitcase, a garment bag, and overnight bag for toiletries.

"Sorry it took so long."

"No problem. We better get going though, if you still wanna go out tonight." *Please say no, please say no.* "I highly recommend changing your mind."

"No way. I need to go out now, more than ever."

She walked out, leaving him no choice but to follow.

Chapter Nine

Sloane

Sloane hung her garment bag on the back of the closet door in Max's spare room. Unzipping it, she pulled the fabric free of the plastic casing. She didn't want her clothes to have a plastic smell. She recovered her robe from the suitcase, then checked the hall before exiting the room. No Max. She hustled over to the bathroom and locked the door behind her. After stripping quickly, she stepped under the hot spray coming from the showerhead. She took her time washing her hair and her body.

When she was sufficiently clean, she toweled off, wrapped her robe around herself like a suit of armor, and exited the bathroom prepared to sprint to her room. No luck, however. When she opened the door, Max was leaning up against the wall adjacent to the bathroom with his arms crossed over his muscular chest, waiting for his turn. *Yummy*. Damn, she was such a loser. *Ugh*.

"It's all yours," she called on her way down the

hall. No way was she going to turn around to face him.

With the dresser now covered in cosmetics and hair products, she set about the task of transforming herself. She was a single gal now, after all. She could do whatever, or whomever, she wanted to. It was a liberating feeling. She wondered what it would be like to do Max Fear. Sloane quickly pushed that idea aside, giggling to herself. She was halfway through applying her makeup when Max called to her from the other side of the door.

"Um...hey, I've got something to do, so Foster and Bella will be here to get you in less than a half hour."

"Oh...okay." She tried not to sound disappointed. Why the hell should she care? She shouldn't. She did.

"I won't be long. I gotta pick up a friend and I'll be there right after you guys."

He had to pick up a *date*. Wonder if he remembered his handcuffs. What would it be like to be handcuffed and left to his mercy? Not that she cared. *Stupid man.* With renewed resolve, she finished applying her eye shadow. The dark smoky eyes looked hot even to her.

After her makeup was done, she slipped on her black tube dress. She'd purchased it a few months ago. Sadly, she hadn't yet had a chance to wear it. Her breasts were a little too large to go completely braless, but a strapless did the trick without ruining the look. The red three-inch heels helped along her five-foot, five-inch frame. It didn't hurt that they made her legs look fantastic. Which was a definite plus considering how much of them were exposed.

Stepping onto the back porch, she did a slow turn for Mirabella and Foster as they waited in his Tahoe. It was a lot tighter and shorter than anything that she had ever worn before. She was actually nervous about wearing it. Bella squealed in delight while Foster gave appreciative catcalls. She was smiling in a way she hadn't in days—hell, in months. She needed this more than she'd realized. Carefully, she made her way down the steps and folded herself inside Foster's SUV and off they went.

The club wasn't packed yet, but there was a decent enough crowd. Sloane glanced around, taking everything in. The bar itself took up a large portion of the room. Placed in the middle of the large space, it was definitely the focal point of the room. Tables spread out all around the room with multiple booths hugging the dark walls. A loud whistle caught her attention. She didn't recognize the trio of men there, but apparently Foster did. He waved to them as he headed in their direction. Bella and Sloane let him lead the way.

"Guys, this is my fiancée, Mirabella, and this is her cousin, Sloane."

The girls shook hands with the guys as Foster finished introducing them, giving their real names before informing they preferred nicknames. Paxton, or "Tank," was just that—a huge man whose hand swallowed Sloane's with room to spare. The shaved head only added to the magnitude of him. He wore a loud orange button-down shirt that couldn't hide all of his tattoos, with black jeans and motorcycle boots. His large brown eyes swept the room, constantly alert. As if constantly looking for some presumed threat. She knew she wouldn't want to be on the other end of that stare.

Morty "Mother" must have been half of Tank's size, with what she could only describe as hipster black-framed glasses covering his gray eyes. His t-shirt matched his eyes almost perfectly. She almost laughed out loud after spying his white sneakers poking out beneath his blue jeans. He looked like the kind of guy who was more comfortable hanging out in local coffee houses for hours on end in front of a laptop or with a book in his hand.

When Sloane got to Kasper, more affectionately known as "Gutter Mouth," the name alone made her laugh. Blue eyes sparkled right back at her, and a cocky smirk crossed his face. His blond hair ended just above his chin; it looked so soft she almost asked to touch it. A crimson shirt pulled taut across his shoulders showcased a lean, muscled body underneath. Unlike Mother, his wasn't tucked into his dark-wash jeans. He was hot, to say the least.

"Sloane, I've gotta say it. You look fuckin' hot in that dress. Dayum."

He took her hand and kissed the top of it. With that simple move, he had the capacity to both put her on edge and at ease, all at the same time. She felt heat blossom in her cheeks. Foster and Bella laughed at something Tank said as they pulled up chairs next to where she stood.

"Come on, Darlin', sit down next to me. Unless you'd rather sit in my lap?" Kasper waggled his eyebrows.

"Gutter Mouth, behave," Foster pretended to chastise him. Everyone laughed. "Watch that one, Sloane. He's trouble."

"Foster, you wound me, man." Kasper winked across the table.

Sloane sat there listening to the men tell stories of old times before Foster met Bella. Eventually she began to feel restless. The strawberry margaritas were fabulous. Every sweet, sugary sip pulled a little more of the tension she was feeling from her. They hadn't been there long and she was already on her third one.

Evanescence boomed through the speaker, and the pulsing beat pulled on her. She was on her feet before she realized it, heading for the dance floor. Her hips swayed to the music that was breathing life back into her.

Sloane stayed near the edge of the dance floor; she didn't want to have to fight her way through the crowd and this way Foster and Bella could see her at all times, per their agreement. She was enjoying the music, dancing with a muscle-bound, brown-haired man to her left and a tattoo-covered man with his head shaved clean to her right. Both men took her in, undressing her with their eyes, but neither of them touched her anywhere inappropriately. The way she was beginning to feel, she may have welcomed it.

Halfway through the song, warm hands encased her hips, moving in sync with her. She didn't move them, allowing her new dance partner to press his body flush with hers. The rich musky scent of his cologne was nice—not overpowering like the kind a lot of men used. Kasper spun her around and wrapped his arms around her. His body pressed to hers tightly. The other two men forgotten, she smiled up at him. Feeling the eyes of everyone at their table, she risked a look over while never losing the rhythm they had created.

The only face she was able to make out was Max's. Like a statue, he stood absolutely still, his eyes glued to the dance floor. No, not just the dance floor, but on her and Kasper specifically. She noticed a leggy redhead had her arm entwined with his.

She was pretty and it bugged the shit out of Sloane. Why couldn't she have been wrong? Would it have hurt to have the girl look less like a model and more like say, a troll? Then again, this was Max. He was gorgeous. He could have any woman in the room.

Secretly, Sloane wished he wanted her. He knew Brody. She had to keep that in mind. God only knows what Brody told him about her. No doubt what a lousy sexual partner she was. Why would Max want to waste his time with someone like her?

Forget it, she berated herself. She was currently in the arms of a hot guy. A hot guy who definitely *did* want her, even if it was only for tonight. She was fine with that. More than fine. That's what she wanted—some mindless fun, and she was going to enjoy every second of it. Sloane turned her attention back to Kasper, rolling her body down his.

Two more dance songs played before the DJ slowed it down. She was ready to sit down, and luckily it seemed Kasper had read her mind. A light sheen of sweat glistened on her skin. She couldn't wait to get back to her frozen margarita. Kasper took her hand loosely, leading her back to the table. It was a sweet, yet possessive gesture.

"Max! Good to see you again, man. Who's your friend?" Kasper slapped Max's hand in lieu of a normal handshake.

"Charlie, this is Kasper and Sloane."

"Hi guys. You two make a really cute couple." Charlie smiled. Kasper pulled Sloane off the chair she was sitting in and into his lap, ripping an unexpected squeal from her.

"We do, don't we, Darlin'?" He winked at her. Sloane watched Charlie rub her hand down Max's chest.

"Sure do, Cowboy," Sloane answered as she wrapped her arms around Kasper's neck.

***

Max

What. The. Fuck. Did he miss while picking up Charlie and why did he care so much? He knew why—because Sloane looked like a fucking goddess on the dance floor. That sad excuse for a dress clinging to every single curve on her mouthwatering body was like a second skin. Every unattached male in there had their eyes glued to her tits or her ass, neither of which were properly covered.

He'd wanted to drag her off the dance floor the moment he'd laid eyes on her. Those two strange men had been stealing touches wherever they could. They were nothing, however, compared to the way Gutter Mouth had been touching her. Now she was sitting there in his lap laughing like he was the funniest man alive. Why the hell was she calling him "Cowboy"? Now that he thought about it, he didn't like him calling her "Darlin'" either.

Charlie cleared her throat beside him. No, he hadn't forgotten her "cute couple" comment either. They did *not* look cute together. She was too…and he was too…They just weren't cute together. This evening was not going the way he had envisioned. Here he thought he would spend a few hours watching out for Sloane before taking Charlie back to her house, where he would fuck her senseless before returning home himself.

Maybe if Sloane had kept dancing with the strangers it would've been different. If it hadn't been Kasper's hands sliding down her back, gripping her waist as he pushed himself against her, maybe it wouldn't be affecting him this way. No, it didn't matter who touched her. He didn't like it. Not one single bit. She was his. She just didn't know it yet.

"Max told me you ran into some trouble at work," Charlie said to Sloane in between Kasper's ever-witty jokes. His fingertips roved lazily across Sloane's bare knee. Bastard.

"Yeah, I was in the right place at the wrong time. The guys have been worried about me ever since. And to make matters worse, my apartment was broken into."

"Oh my God! How horrible. I couldn't imagine

88

going back to something like that. It makes my skin crawl just thinking about it."

"It's scary and I felt violated after seeing my apartment, that's for sure. Now I'm on lockdown until he's caught or the guys think I'm safe."

"I'll keep you safe, Darlin'." If Gutter Mouth didn't stop winking at Sloane that way, Max was going to lose his shit. He was already hanging on by a thread with the way he was touching her.

"Aww, how romantic. Like a white knight. How long have you two been dating?"

"We aren't, actually. We just met tonight," Sloane said, jabbing Kasper with a playful elbow to the side.

"Oh wow, really? I'm sorry. I just assumed."

"See what happens when you assume?" Max growled.

"Anyway—" Charlie gave him a disapproving look. "—it at least helps to know guys like these are looking out for you, right?"

Sloane sighed. "It does, but I'll be happy once it's all over. I just want to get on with my life. I hate living out of a suitcase."

"Have you been staying at a hotel?" Charlie asked.

"Um, actually I've been staying with Max."

Charlie's eyes widened for a fraction of a second; only someone studying her reaction would have noticed it. Max knew she'd want an explanation of some sort, but she wasn't his girlfriend, and he didn't want her to think she was by giving her one. She'd never been his girlfriend. She did, however, know his number one rule: No women at his home.

"Oh. Well I hope you'll be okay."

"I'll be fine," Sloane said. She lied almost as well as Bella, he thought.

The night went by slowly for Max. Every time Sloane and Kasper hit the dance floor, Max wanted to hit *him*. Charlie asked him to dance several times, but he couldn't be bothered. In fact, he wished she would stop pawing all over him. He wasn't a touchy feely in public kind of guy. Then again, he wasn't a touchy feely guy in private either. Sure, he had no problem touching a woman. He could work Charlie with ease, but he wasn't the kind of guy to cuddle with after or talk about feelings. Why the hell did he bring her here in the first place? Oh yeah, he wanted to get laid. What a joke.

Talk about a touchy feely man. Now Kasper had his hands just above the soft globes of her ass as the song ended. With each song his hands dropped lower. One or two songs more and he would have Sloane's sweet ass in the palms of his grimy hands, literally. A slow pop song sang about love. It was the first slow song that they had danced to. Sloane put her head on Gutter Mouth's shoulder, eliminating any space between them. Max saw red. Oh hell no, he wasn't going to sit and watch this.

Max was on his feet before common sense could stop him. He tapped Kasper on the shoulder, and without a word he stepped in, taking his place. Surprise washed over Sloane's features before she could school her expression. What did she see when she looked at him? Did his eyes give him away? Did she know what she did to him or how hard he'd

90

fought against her pull? Her arms slipped around his neck, but inches still separated their bodies. He couldn't have that. He needed to erase Kasper from her body.

Max pulled her close enough that he knew she could feel his semi-erection press into her belly. He didn't care; in this moment, he wanted her to know. Her breasts practically flattened between their bodies he held her so tightly. Like a lover's caress, his hands never stopped moving. Sliding down her back, up her side, swirling circles on her hip. Her arms were wrapped around his shoulders. One hand played with the hair on the nape of his neck. Their eyes locked together, unwavering. It was breathtaking.

The song continued on as the rest of the room fell away. No one else existed. Sight, sound, smell—all of his senses were filled with only her. His hands threaded into her golden mane, pulling her head forward to meet his. Their bodies touched from their foreheads, chests, and hips. He could taste her breath on his lips as they swayed together. The sweet smell of the margaritas she had been drinking beckoned to him to take a taste.

He was just about to give in and take that taste when suddenly Sloane pulled away, her eyes wide with wonder. Max instantly missed the feel of her. Cold seeped into his skin all the while his blood burned for her. He wanted to grab her again and beg her not to let go this time.

"Song's over," she whispered like he cared.

"Just like that, it's over..." Max didn't know if he was making a statement or asking a question.

Was he talking about the dance or the enchantment they had been under? That he was *still* under? She opened her mouth, an answer on the tip of her tongue. Max held his breath, waiting for her reply. Whatever she said could make or break this thing he could feel between them. Meanwhile, the DJ was taking his sweet time announcing the next song. Max wished she'd answer before the music drowned her out.

"Hey, Darlin' get your sweet ass over here." From the table Kasper's loud call pulled her attention away from Max.

"Gutter Mouth, shut the fuck up."

It was out of Max's mouth before he could stifle it. He groaned internally, slowly closing his eyes in frustration. *Way to lose your cool there, Maxwell.* Sloane's jaw dropped slightly. It might have been comical in any other situation. Risking a look behind him, Max took in the expressions on his friends' faces. Disbelief, humor, self-righteousness, and—yup, right there to round it all out—rage. Charlie was one pissed off woman.

That pissed off woman was heading in his direction, a murderous look in her eye. Her confident stride quickly ate up the space between them. Briefly he wondered if he could hide behind Sloane. Nah, even in her incredibly sexy heels she was still a few inches shorter than him.

"You had to be here to *protect* her?" she accused, her hands waving around.

He wanted to say yes, that's exactly why he was here, but he couldn't get the words out. The whole drive to Charlie's house he kept thinking of the way

Sloane's ass had looked under the robe she was wearing as she ran to her room. He should have known this night wouldn't end well.

"Looks to me like Kasper had things under control just fine without you."

"Charlie—"

"No. Just no, Max."

***

Sloane

Sloane watched Charlie march back to their table to collect her purse. She eyed Sloane, shaking her head in disapproval. What the hell did she do now?

"Look, Charlie…" He tried to talk to her, but she wasn't having it.

"Handcuffs, Max…Hope she's worth it."

For the second time in less than five minutes, Sloane was frozen with her mouth hanging open. Peering up at Max, she tried but couldn't read his expression. What the hell just happened? One minute she's having a great time flirting with Kasper and seriously thinking of letting him take her home, the next she's lost in a moment so intense with Max, she forgot where she was.

Perhaps Charlie's departure was a good time to call it a night. Max refused to meet her gaze, so she left him standing there on the edge of the dance floor. She tried to ignore the looks from everyone. She was just as confused to the cause of Max's outburst as they were. She just shrugged her shoulders.

93

"It looks like the party is over tonight, Darlin'."

"So it does." Sloane put on the happiest face she could muster. It wasn't much.

"So, you gonna let me call you?"

"Sure, I'd like that."

She smiled for real this time. How could she not when Kasper flashed that sexy as sin grin? Sloane knew he was probably a total player, but she didn't care. It wasn't as if she was looking for forever. She just wanted some fun, so she gave him her cell phone number. After hugging everyone goodbye, she promised them they would all get together again. Sloane picked up her clutch, trailing out behind Mirabella. She was just about to get in the Tahoe when Max called out to her.

"Sloane, I'm over here."

"I see that."

"I mean, why are you getting in Foster's SUV?"

"He was driving me home. As per your request."

"Why would he go out of his way to drive you when I'm here and going to the same place? That makes no sense. Get your ass in the truck."

"Fine," she mumbled, walking to his truck. "Night, guys," she called back.

"Hey, darlin'," Kasper bellowed while running toward her across the parking lot.

He was crouched down to half his height, closing the distance between them quickly. He was ex-SWAT and she could easily imagine him in action. All he needed was his gear.

He picked her up without slowing his speed, spinning them around in circles until she was dizzy. Considering the amount of alcohol she had consumed, it didn't take long before she was yelling and giggling.

He stopped abruptly, letting her body slowly slide down his until her feet hit the ground. The friction caused her dress to slide up enough that only the swell of her ass stopped her from an indecent exposure charge. She tried to tug it back down as Kasper grabbed her face. He pressed a soft, closed-mouth kiss to her lips, winking when he stepped away.

"I'll hit you up later, beautiful."

"See ya around, cowboy."

She couldn't hide the smile on her face as she hoisted herself up into Max's truck. Which was not easy considering her attire. He barely gave her time to shut the door before he sped off out of the parking lot. *Whoa.* What was his deal? Up until the end, she'd had a great night. She met some new people who helped take her mind off of all her problems for a little while. Sloane could have done without seeing Max with Charlie, but it wasn't any of her business who Max slept with. The chaste kiss from Kasper probably would have been amazing, if only she hadn't had Max as the new standard of kisses. That was a depressing thought.

Max parked the truck and then exited without saying a word. *Whatever.* She wasn't in the mood to deal with him anyway. Her plans of getting laid were ruined. Maybe she still could've went home with Kasper. If only she had his number, he could come get her. She'd only given him hers, though. Asking Max for it didn't sound like a good idea. Foster, maybe. Yeah, that's a better plan, but it would have to wait. Now that she'd taken her shoes off, she realized she wasn't going anywhere. Max slammed the refrigerator door, startling her.

"What's your problem? You're acting like you have a huge bug up your ass."

"The only problem I have is trying to keep you safe," he growled. "Going to a crowded club with wall to wall strangers was a bad idea."

Sloane folded her arms. "Foster didn't seem to think so."

"That's because Foster was thinking of keeping Bella happy. I was thinking of keeping *you* alive."

Sloane didn't know what to say. She was so angry with him for ruining her night and yet at the same time she understood what he was saying. She knew he was trying to look after her. The whole situation sucked. She hated being babysat. She hated being a burden on him. She decided she didn't want to fight with him.

"Do you mind if I shower first? All that dancing made me sweaty."

"No, go ahead."

"Thank you. Good night."

"Night."

Sloane wanted to press him. She wanted to ask if keeping her safe was all that was on his mind. He was pissed at her. She couldn't bring herself to ask, though. She didn't want him to tell her how he screwed up with Charlie. Ignorance is bliss. On the dance floor with his arms around her was by far the most sensual encounter that she'd had in...well, ever. Like a ray of sunlight, it warmed her, bringing with it desire like she'd never known. Her panties were still damp with it.

She stripped everything off and stepped into the shower. She poured body wash into her hand, lathering herself. Her palms moved smoothly over her breasts, the nipples peeking into stiff points. She closed her eyes. She remembered the way they pressed into Max's hard chest, not even an hour ago. There was something about Maxwell Fear that pushed every one of her buttons. She massaged her hands down her body, picturing Max there with her. She imagined him holding her from behind.

Sliding her hand down lower, her fingers touched the delicate folds between her thighs. Skimming them gently, she shivered. Placing one foot on the side of the tub, she let her head fall back, giving into the sensations overwhelming her body. The water continued to rinse away the rest of the suds as she plunged her finger inside. Already the digit was slick with her juices. Sloane pulled it out before pushing back in, adding another finger this time. In and out she drove them repeatedly. Soft moans escaped her, even as she bit down on her bottom lip to stop it. The pressure, building rapidly. Her hips rocked forward on their own accord, fighting for sweet release.

She imagined Max's hands on her like they were on the dance floor. The feel of his breath in her face. She imagined they were still there dancing. That they were his fingers bringing her closer. Not caring who witnessed their performance.

It hit her hard and fast. Her inner walls squeezed her fingers as she cried out. It almost had her collapsing on the shower floor. Using the tile wall to hold her up, she waited until the aftershocks subsided before rinsing herself yet again. Finally, exhausted, she wrapped herself in a towel. She hustled to her room, dropping the towel at her feet before collapsing onto the bed.

***

Max

The entire drive home, all Max could see was the image of Gutter Mouth pressing his lips to Sloane's. He couldn't even say anything, for crying out loud. He'd had Charlie there for no reason other than to fuck her afterward. He was so pissed he could hardly see straight. Now might be a good time to ask her what was going on with them, but what if he didn't like the answer? What if she was interested in Gutter Mouth for real? He hoped she was just flirting to have some fun. For now, he had to try to ignore it. He wished he could ignore the way she felt in his arms.

Once Sloane was in the shower, he checked his messages. Nothing but a few solicitors, thankfully. This whole mess started with checking his messages. He was worn out. He needed to stretch out in bed and get some much-needed rest. His emotions were all over the place. He wasn't used to feeling this way, but something about her called to him.

Climbing the stairs, he heard a moan. His body instantly on alert, he pulled his gun from his waistband, stopping outside the bathroom door. No way, she couldn't be. Yet, there it was again. A soft moan. She was in *his* shower getting herself off while he stood in the hallway like a dirty pervert listening.

His cock grew hard quickly. It was almost painful as it strained in an odd angle against his zipper. He reached down to adjust himself, trying to alleviate the ache. Another moan, more intense now. He swiftly began undoing the button on his jeans. Tugging the zipper down and releasing himself into his hand, he began to work his cock. He spread the bead of pre-cum down his shaft, stroking himself to the sound of Sloane's pleasure.

Max wished he was in there with her. He imagined covering every inch of her sweet ivory flesh with his lips. He kept his pace slow, only increasing the grip and strength of each pull. His breathing grew shallower with each pump of his wrist. Like a deviant, he pressed his forehead to the bathroom door. It reminded him of the way he'd pressed it against Sloane's at the club. The way her eyes had been glued to him as he'd learned her body with his hands.

The urgency in her murmurs increased. He was close. Reaching behind him, he pulled his t-shirt off with his other hand and positioned it to catch the mess he was about to create. She cried out loudly, pushing him over the edge. Thick tendrils of cum spurted from him onto his shirt. As soon as he was done, he moved—as quickly as he could—to his room. He left the door open a crack to watch her move from one room to the next. Her face was flushed, nothing except a big fluffy gray towel covering her. She swayed with physical exhaustion. He made up his mind right then and there. Her next orgasm would belong to him.

Chapter Ten

Sloane

Morning was not a friend to Sloane. Her tongue was stuck to the roof of her mouth while a freight train barreled through her head. *Ugh.* Why oh why did she drink that last margarita? She rolled out of bed slowly. She was still naked from when she crawled—or fell—into bed last night. Quickly, or as quickly as she could in her condition, she haphazardly pulled on a blue tank top and a pair of plaid flannel sleep shorts. She found Max in the kitchen, head hanging over a coffee mug that smelled absolutely fantastic.

Her cheeks heated with the memory of her self-induced release, with the sexy Max Fear as her inspiration. He never even bothered to raise his head to acknowledge her existence. So at least he wouldn't wonder what was going on with her rosy cheeks. *Whatever.* All she wanted was a cup of that steaming life elixir to help put her head on straight. A half dozen aspirin wouldn't hurt either.

Not wanting to break the silence, Sloane moved around the kitchen stealthily collecting what she needed for a perfect cup of Joe. Like she wasn't even there, Max got off the stool, washed out his mug, and placed it in the dishwasher. Sloane was just about to ask him what his problem was when he walked out of the room. No way was she gonna hang around here today. She felt unwanted, like an intruder. She wasn't going to stay where she wasn't wanted. Maybe she'd call Bella later and take her up on her offer.

Twenty minutes later, she was dressed with a minimal amount of makeup on. Max was nowhere in sight. She stopped to listen at the basement steps. She could hear music accompanied by the clink of weights. She almost felt bad about going through his kitchen drawers, but she was quickly rewarded with her prize in the second one opened. She removed the pen and notepad and jotted down a quick note, pinning it to the fridge under a magnet for a local pizza delivery joint. When he came up for water, he was certain to see it.

The cab pulled up out front about ten minutes later. Sloane didn't waste any time running out to it. Jumping inside, she gave the driver her destination. She would have taken her own car, but her keys were missing and she couldn't find them. She felt like a teenager sneaking out after she had been grounded. She sat in the back seat of the cab grinning. The cab driver probably thought she was a moron. *Oh well.*

First stop, the mall. Retail therapy was in order. She wandered through the stores looking for nothing in particular. She didn't need lingerie, since she no longer had a man to wear it for. She didn't need anything for the apartment, because she wasn't sure when she could go back. Work clothes seemed ridiculous, since she had no idea what would happen to her job.

She needed to decide what to do. Since Detlef was no longer around, she figured her job no longer existed. She could get by for a little while, though—she was always smart with money. She had a healthy balance in her savings, and a nice investment portfolio started, in case of an emergency. That would be tomorrow's problem. She continued window-shopping until her growling stomach reminded her it was almost lunch. She'd skipped breakfast in her hurry to get out of Max's house. At least her headache was somewhat manageable now, but she knew it wouldn't stay that way if she didn't eat something soon.

With her one new outfit swinging in a bag—jeans that hugged her ass and a cute new top—she made her way over to the food court. Enjoying her turkey club sandwich, she sat and people watched. She was just finishing her food when her purse started to ring by her feet. She bent over to retrieve her phone from the bag. She was unlocking the screen when pain exploded in her shoulder.

Crying out, she dropped the phone. It hit the table before falling on the floor. She pressed a hand to her left shoulder as liquid fire burned through her muscles. People screamed and pointed at her, their eyes wide in horror. Sloane glanced down, and there was blood oozing down her arm. *What the hell?*

A large crack! echoed in the air and chunks of plastic burst from the table only an inch from her body. Someone was shooting. At *her*.

Sloane dropped under the table, picking up the phone from where it'd landed. She had to call Max. She looked down at the screen. The front was completely shattered and had gone dark; she couldn't get it to dial out. *Shit*. This was bad. This was really bad.

***

Max

Max was beyond pissed. He glowered before the fridge, reading Sloane's short handwritten note for the third time. Each time he read it only added to his anger.

Max,

Going out for a while. Don't worry; I'll watch my back. Need to take care of a few things. I may drop by the apartment too. It's doubtful I'll be back before dinner, so don't feel you need to stick around.

Sloane

How could she just leave? Max had warned her it wasn't safe to be out by herself. What the hell was she thinking going back to her apartment? The woman was exhausting. Not even bothering with a shower, Max pulled on a pair of cargo shorts followed by a black polo shirt and his shoes. He raced out to his truck. He had hoped to avoid this scenario by putting her car keys on top of his fridge out of her reach.

Three times he called her phone, and each time it went to voicemail. *Son of a bitch*. After coming to a screeching halt in front of her apartment building, Max forwent the elevator, running up the five flights of stairs. He pounded on her door, repeatedly calling her name.

"Sloane?"

A young woman next door poked her head out. When she saw Max, she straightened her shirt, rolling her shoulders back to lift her breasts up. She played with the ends of her hair while exiting her apartment. He wasn't impressed.

"She isn't there. Hasn't been all day," she cooed. "If you want, you can wait in my apartment."

"No thanks, Ma'am."

Max bolted back down the stairs. In his truck again, he called Foster. The moment Foster said hello, Max went off on a tirade laced with worry. "Have you or Bella heard from her?"

"No, man. What's going on?"

Max told Foster about the note he'd found after his workout. "I'm surprised she didn't call," Foster said. "I'm sure she just needed some space. Last night was pretty intense."

Max shook his head. "I got a bad feeling."

"I'm sure it's nothing. You try Gutter Mouth? Maybe he heard from her. They were pretty cozy most of the night. I thought she might even...you

105

know…until you stepped in…" He trailed off.

Max gritted his teeth. "No, I haven't tried him yet. I had hoped she'd come to you guys." He didn't want to picture her holed up with Gutter Mouth somewhere. His stomach soured.

"What the hell happened last night? I'm surprised the sparks flying between you two didn't set the place ablaze."

"Dude, I don't even know how to explain it."

"Charlie was pissed. It would take some major groveling to even hope she might forgive you after that scene." Max could hear the humor laced in Foster's voice.

"I'm not worried about Charlie; it wasn't ever more than a friendly fuck with her. Neither of us wanted anything serious."

"I didn't get that vibe from Charlie, but whatever, man. I'll make some calls. If I hear from Sloane, I'll let you know. I'll tell Bella too."

"Thanks."

Max hung up. He'd already checked her apartment. No way would she go to her office. She wasn't with her cousin. Cringing, Max dialed the phone. Gripping the steering wheel harder, he waited for the ringing to stop.

"Yeah, man?" Gutter Mouth's lazy drawl had him gripping the wheel even tighter still.

"Have you seen Sloane?"

"No. Wait, I thought she was with you."

"She did a skip while I was working out."

"I texted her a few times, but she never replied. I thought maybe she was brushing me off. I couldn't sleep last night, so I did a little digging into the name you gave me. According to the description she gave and the name she heard, I think I found one of our guys. Milo Booker is a mid-level thug that works for the Petrov family."

"Fuck. Russian Mob. This just keeps getting better and better."

The Petrov family was notorious for every type of felony under the sun. From jury tampering, to drug and human trafficking, to good old-fashioned murder. Wonderful, just fucking wonderful. Max punched his steering wheel. He didn't know where he was going. Now he was driving around town in circles.

"If my sources are correct, the other guy may be Viktor Runikov. Petrov's number two."

"Any more shitty news for me?" Max barked through the phone.

"Her boss was into some shady shit with these guys, Max. You know as well as I do, it doesn't take much for them to see you as a liability and exterminate you."

Max sighed. "I know."

"Sorry, dude."

"This is a complete clusterfuck. I didn't think I'd have to actually babysit her so she wouldn't run off. She has no idea what she's up against."

"Sloane can always stay here if she's too much of a hassle for you." The barely contained excitement in Kasper's voice pissed him off even more.

"She's fine right where she is. Can you trace her phone?"

"I'm not a tech guru like Mother, but I can run a

simple trace."

"Good. I can't believe she isn't answering. Why the fuck isn't she answering her goddamn phone?"

"Um…We might not need the trace. Where you at, dude?"

"Circling town. Why?"

"If you're near the mall, they just reported shots fired on the police scanner. Something tells me that might be our girl."

Max hung up without saying goodbye. "Our girl," his ass. He busted an illegal U-turn going as fast as he dared to get to the mall. He parked in the first open spot, not caring that it was marked as handicapped. Running toward the cop cars and ambulances, Max spied a gurney being wheeled out. Sloane. Pushing his way through the crowd, he slipped past the beat cop keeping the looky loos back.

Her eyes were closed. He didn't think it was possible, but her skin was even paler than usual. The paramedics kept up their hurried pace to the ambulance, lifting the gurney quickly. Max tried to climb in after them.

"Sorry sir, only family allowed in the ambulance. You can meet us at Mercy General."

No way was Max letting her out of his sight again. Not when the Petrov family had their sights on *her*. "I'm her fiancé. Please."

"Okay then, but stay out of our way." The man glared.

The vehicle started moving. The paramedic checked the monitors, repeatedly taking notes.

"How bad is it? Is she going to be okay?"

"She'll be fine. The bullet grazed her upper arm pretty good. Basically ripped a chunk out of her arm. It'll hurt for a while, but the scar left will be the only real damage. She was in shock first and then hysterics so we felt it best to sedate her."

Max breathed a sigh of relief. "Thank God." He couldn't take something happening to her.

***

Sloane

Opening her eyes, Sloane first noticed the bed had handrails. Her bed didn't have rails. It took her foggy brain a few long moments to register it wasn't her bed or Max's guest bed that she had been occupying as of late, but a hospital bed. She shot up straight, looking around.

Max was dozing in an extremely uncomfortable looking chair. His face was relaxed. He looked peaceful, his hair slightly mussed up. She couldn't fathom ever tiring of his face. The man was so damn good looking. She inhaled sharply from the pain in her shoulder. Max opened his eyes.

"Hey, you're awake. How are you feeling?"

"Like I was shot." She smiled.

"It was a deep graze. It should heal well. They had to sedate you at the scene. Seems you were rambling and hysterical. Imagine that."

"Yeah, well I was *shot*." Barking at him wouldn't help, but she couldn't help herself. "How long have I been here?"

"A few hours. They wanna keep you for

observations tonight, but first thing in the morning I should be able to take you home. What the hell were you thinking, Sloane?"

She bit her lip and glanced down at her hands. "I just needed to get out of the house."

"This isn't a game. You could have been killed, Sloane."

The nurse came in to check her vitals, scratching things into a chart at the end of the bed.

"Good evening, Ms. Robertson. How are you feeling?"

"I'm doing okay."

"You are a very lucky woman. Your fiancé hasn't left your side a single minute." She beamed at Max. The way she was looking at him began to grate on Sloane's nerves. She was apparently his fiancée—when the hell did that happen? Even though the nurse said the right words to Sloane, her eyes were begging Max to make a move.

"You haven't?" Sloane asked, more to make conversation while she stewed, not because she doubted it.

"I needed to be sure you were okay." Shrugging, he looked down at his hands that hung between his knees.

"I tried to get him to go to the cafeteria to eat. No matter what I offered, he refused to leave."

Max looked up at the nurse, his eyes slightly wider than usual. Nurse Trampy licked her lips slower than what was necessary. The bitch was blatantly flirting with him right in front of Sloane. She just bet he knew what the tart was offering, and it sure as shit wasn't food in the cafeteria. Sloane couldn't believe her gall. Maybe it was the effects of the drugs still lingering in her system, or maybe it was something else she wasn't ready to admit, but she decided to nip this shit in the bud.

"Aww, Max." Sloane held her hand out to him. With a wary expression, he stood and walked over to the bed. The slut nurse stepped into him "accidentally." Her breast brushed his arm while she checked Sloane's vital readouts on the screens yet again. *That's it.* As soon as Max sat on the edge of the bed, Sloane wrapped her hand behind his neck and pulled him down to her.

She claimed his lips like she had done it a million times. Like she knew his body intimately. She dragged her hand up the back of his neck into his hair. Sloane quickly found herself so lost in the kiss, she forgot she was simply trying to make her point to the nurse. She mewled her pleasure into his mouth. His hand squeezed her hip as the other braced himself above her. Sloane's entire body ignited. Max kissed like he could read her mind.

A throat clearing from the door released her from the spell she was under. Sloane pulled away, looking toward the hall. Foster and Bella stood there with identical smirks on their faces. The nurse was nowhere to be seen.

"Hey, guys!" Sloane straightened herself, sitting up further. Max flashed her a look she didn't understand. Then he walked away from her. Guess he didn't like her ruining his chances with Nurse Slut. *Whoops.* Bella smiled, rushing to her side.

"Honey, are you really okay?"

"Yes."

"We were so worried. Why would you run out like that?"

"I wasn't running out. I went shopping. I needed some time to think. I really just needed to be alone."

Even to Sloane's own ears it sounded like a lame excuse. Her whining made her sound like a child.

A tap at the door had them all turning to look at the new arrivals. Kasper and Tank waltzed inside, and Max turned back to the window, tension evident in his stance. His arms were crossed in front of his chest, his feet planted shoulder width apart. It didn't take him more than a minute to turn around to face them all, and then the tension was magically gone. Either she'd imagined it or he was a hell of an actor. An incredibly sexy actor. With an amazingly talented mouth.

"Hey there, Darlin'."

"Hey there yourself, Cowboy." Sloane smiled. "Hey Tank. What are you guys doing here?"

Tank shoved his massive hands into his pockets. His voice barely more than a whisper, he murmured, "We were worried about you."

"You were?" She couldn't help the surprise in her voice. She couldn't imagine the giant standing before her worried about anything, much less her.

"Max mentioned what you're dealing with; we thought we'd see if we could help," Kasper added. Tank nodded as if they had agreed to a deal, but she had no idea what.

Kasper moved closer, kissed her cheek, and flashed his signature smile. He leaned back down, whispering in her ear so softly she knew no one else could hear.

"Ever fuck in a hospital bed, Darlin'?"

"Get outta here." She slapped him playfully in the arm while shaking her head, still laughing.

"Back the fuck up, Gutter Mouth," Max snarled.

"Dude, what the fuck is your problem?"

"She's *my* fiancée."

Everyone stared at Max like he'd grown a second head before he recovered. "I mean, I had to tell everyone Sloane was my fiancée so they would let me stay with her. It would look shady as fuck if someone walked in and saw the two of you just now. You know what I mean?" He looked knowingly at Sloane.

Sloane frowned. "Max is right. It would look awful. I apologize, Max."

***

Max

If Max was in his right mind he would remain where he was. Keep the distance between them, but he wasn't. The kiss she'd laid on him before everyone arrived left every neuron firing inside him. Seeing her flirt with Kasper only added to the possessiveness he was feeling. He did not like the idea that she could be attracted to Kasper. Or anyone other than him, for that matter.

Which was stupid because he didn't do relationships. He hadn't in years. Not since he decided to join the force. He had to get control over himself.

"Sorry, man, it's just important to keep up

pretenses. I need to be able to stay here to keep her safe. The Petrov family is no joke."

"I get it, dude. No problem."

"Petrov family?" Sloane's eyes widened.

"It's gonna be fine."

"Yeah, Darlin'. We won't let anything happen to you."

"I've got feelers out. A few leads have trickled in as to Booker's whereabouts," Tank added.

"See, nothing for you to worry about. Having said that, I need you to listen to me. When I give you an order I expect it followed. No going out alone."

"I'm sorry," she whispered.

Max wandered over to the bed, lowering himself down next to her. He started rubbing his hand up and down Sloane's blanket-covered thigh. He ignored everyone else in the room except Gutter Mouth. Max hoped he was making his silent claim clear. Gutter Mouth needed to stay away from Sloane. Gutter Mouth raised a questioning eyebrow before a mischievous smirk played over the corner of his lips. Just in case Gutter Mouth wasn't catching on to his seriousness, Max maneuvered himself in the bed so he was stretched out beside her.

That's how the flirtatious nurse, Alley, found them when she returned. For that alone, Max was grateful that he positioned himself where he was. The entire time Sloane was unconscious the petite brunette made it very clear that she wouldn't be missed if she disappeared for twenty minutes. She even told him where the supply closet was.

Honestly, he was worn out from turning down her advances all night. Years ago he might've taken her up on her offer, but he had outgrown nameless one-night stands. He wasn't celibate by any stretch of the imagination, but he kept his options opened to three or four regulars with no promise of anything serious on the horizon.

The reappearance of Nurse Alley speared Sloane into action. She laid her head on his shoulder. Max was careful not to bump her injured arm as he slid his around her. The way she snuggled into him heated his blood. Then it rapidly moved south, causing his pants to tighten slightly. Maybe she would kiss him again. Probably not with everyone else in the room. That disappointed him, but her body pressed into his was enough. For now, that is.

"Visiting hours are over, everyone." Alley's eyes locked on his. They were still full of proposition. No matter how many times he declined, she wouldn't back off. It was an unattractive quality.

"I'm not leaving." Max stared defiantly at her. The kiss he placed on Sloane's forehead punctuated the seriousness behind his words. The act felt completely normal, as if he did it every day in the past and would continue to do so every day in the future.

"Of course, Mr. Fear. Everyone else must leave for the evening. I'll be back in five minutes to check." Alley gave him a disappointed look before turning on her heel and marching out the door.

Bella laughed. "And the plot thickens." A moment of silence shrouded the room and then everyone else joined in.

Everyone finally left after Alley returned for the third time and threatened to call security. Max made no attempt to move. He loved the way Sloane's scent enveloped him. The way her warmth spread into him everywhere they touched. He could get used to this. He realized he wanted to. It didn't take long for her to fall asleep again, this time in his arms. Right where she belonged.

Chapter Eleven

Sloane

The morning couldn't have come sooner. Sloane couldn't wait to get outta this place. Thankfully Nurse Alley was gone with the morning sun. A new nurse with gray hair and a sweet smile checked in on her before going to get the discharge papers. Once Max woke up, he'd removed himself from the bed, walking stiffly to the bathroom. Without saying a word.

She needed a few minutes away from him. She'd woken up multiple times throughout the night. Max was always right there spooned around her. It felt amazing being in his arms, but she knew it wouldn't last. Sloane couldn't afford to let the feeling linger.

Max came out of the bathroom looking slightly more refreshed, his eyes landing on her. Without a word, she averted her eyes and grabbed the bag of her belongings. There was a scrub top left by the day nurse for her to wear home since her shirt had to be cut off. She pushed past him to get dressed in the now vacant bathroom.

Now that a door was between them, she relieved herself before washing her hands and face. She pulled her clothes on quickly, trying to come up with something to say to Max. She'd kissed him last night. Without warning or explanation. She'd just wanted the nurse to stop flirting with him. She didn't know Sloane wasn't really his fiancée and that pissed her off. Who does that? Sloane was shot at, for God's sake, and here some nurse was making a play for her future husband. Well not really, but that was irrelevant.

She knew she couldn't hide in the bathroom all day thinking up the perfect thing to say. She would just go out and apologize for her crass way of dealing with the nurse. She hoped things weren't extremely awkward between them. Stepping out of the bathroom, she was feeling somewhat more energized. Not that she should have worried. The room was empty. She sat in the only chair to put her shoes back on. By the time she was done, Max had returned.

"Are you ready?"

"More than. About last night…"

"Don't worry about it. It was nothing." He brushed her off, walking just ahead of her down the hall.

Nothing? Sloane felt a pang in her chest at his words. She'd kissed him and felt something she had never felt before, but he felt nothing. They stood next to each other, waiting for the elevator doors to open. The ride down to the lobby and the ride to his house were done in silence. She fought to keep her emotions in check. Coming around to the back of Max's farmhouse, she spotted a black Harley Davidson Fat Boy. Max's knuckles turned white as he gripped the steering wheel tighter. Fear momentarily gripped her.

"Is something wrong? Petrov?"

"No, nothing like that."

There was that word again. *Nothing*. Sloane climbed out of the passenger seat, slamming the door closed harder than she really needed to. Damn him for turning her insides into knots. She rounded the bed of the truck, making her way to the house. She watched the gravel crunch under her feet, wondering what to do about staying here with Max. He was too much of a temptation for her. She wanted him too much. Her heart wasn't safe here.

"Hey there, Darlin'."

Her head snapped up. Sitting on the porch stairs with a small black and silver gift bag in one hand and an embarrassingly large bouquet of red roses in the other, was Kasper. He stood up. She ran up to him and wrapped her arms around his neck while kissing his cheek.

"What are you doing here?" Sloane asked as they all walked through the kitchen door.

"Since you aren't engaged to grumpy here anymore, I wanted to bring you an 'I'm sorry you got shot' present." He held up the bouquet of roses and the bag for her to take. She laughed loudly, feeling sincerely happy for the first time since Max had left her in bed alone this morning. "Go on, open it."

Sloane set the flowers down on the counter and

took the bag with both hands. She pulled the tissue paper out, peering into the bag. Inside was a brand new smartphone. It was the same kind she'd had before, only this one was an updated version that didn't have any scratches on the surface like her old one had.

"I already programmed my number in it and your provider can transfer the rest."

"I can't accept this, Kasper."

"Why not?" He looked confused.

"These are hundreds of dollars. I can't let you spend that on me. Let me write you a check for it."

"Fuck no, Darlin'. Money isn't an issue for me. I like to spoil beautiful women, so let me."

"I don't know. I don't feel right taking it. I've never been given a gift like this. Not for any occasion."

"Even more of a reason you should accept it. Plus, I'll just rip up every check you give me." He smirked.

"Fine," Sloane surrendered. "I've never been given a 'Sorry you got shot' present. If I had, I know this would've been the best by far." She giggled.

Max moved around the kitchen slamming cabinets. Finally, he opened the fridge and grabbed a bottle of water. His eyes fixed on Kasper. It looked like he was angry, but she couldn't tell why. If it were any other man, Sloane would say perhaps he was jealous. Since Max made it clear that their kiss was *nothing*, she couldn't figure out what his issue was.

"Hey, Max, do you have something I can put

these in? They're beautiful, by the way. Thank you, Kasper."

Max produced a vase from one of the lower cabinets, setting it on the counter next to where he was standing. She walked around to where he was and started arranging the flowers inside it. "Do you have any aspirin?"

"Are you okay?" He touched her cheek, compelling her attention. His eyes were soft and sincere. Damn, she could get lost in their depths for hours, days, weeks. The way he touched her once again had her wishing he felt something, anything, for her.

"Oh, I'm fine. The pain medicine from the hospital hasn't worn off yet. Adding aspirin to the water prolongs the freshness. It makes the flowers last longer."

"No problem. When they die, I'll buy you fresh ones."

She was more than a little stunned by the chill that resounded in his tone. She stole a glance at Kasper on the other side of the island. He was watching Max, shaking his head slightly in amusement. Did she miss the joke? She took a moment to really look at Kasper. He was dressed in black jeans with a black t-shirt. Celtic looking crosses and skulls adorned the t-shirt, the dark gray color almost camouflaging the design altogether. She just bet he was every women's wet dream dressed like that while riding his Harley.

Not that she was immune to his charms by any means, but when she looked at him next to Max, he paled in comparison. She had fun flirting with

Kasper. She could've even seen herself dating him. He seemed like a great guy. Standing here with both of them, though, made it painfully obvious which man she wanted. Even if he felt nothing.

"So. Whatcha say, Darlin'? You, me, dinner…?"

Before Sloane could respond, however, her non-feeling protector stepped forward. "Not happening."

"Excuse me?" she shrieked in shock. "I don't think that's your decision to make, Max."

Kasper chuckled. "Lady has a point."

"What I meant was…someone tried to kill you yesterday. There's no way you're leaving this house tonight. Plus, Foster and Bella are coming over with dinner."

"Oh…I'm sorry I yelled." She turned to Kasper. "He's right. I really do need to be here if Bella is coming by."

"Sure, no problem. Rain check?" His smile was infectious.

"I'd be wounded if you didn't want one." She winked back at him.

"Hot damn. Then I better get going. Don't let grumpy here get ya down. I'll talk to you later, Beautiful. Later, Maxi Pad."

"Fuck you, Gutter Mouth."

***

Max

It took all Max had not to throw his friend out of his house. The moment Kasper told Sloane she was no longer engaged to him, his temper flared to an almost uncontrollable level. It was ridiculous—they were never engaged. It was a rouse to keep watch over her. So why did it feel so wrong to hear Kasper dismiss it?

He grabbed a bottle of water and chugged it down. Damn he wished it was a beer, but ten in the morning was a little early even for him. He felt more relaxed after Gutter Mouth left.

"I'm going to get cleaned up," Sloane said, wrinkling her nose as she plucked at her scrub top. "I smell like hospital disinfectant. Maybe catch a nap before Foster and Bella get here. Do you mind?"

"Not at all." Max nodded toward her arm. "Try not to get your stitches wet."

Sloane took a step toward him. Her small hand triggered an electrical energy inside him where it rested on his chest. Stretching up on her toes, she kissed his jaw just below his ear. His cock stiffened slightly.

"Thank you, Max. For last night. For the past few days. I really don't know what I would've done without you."

Turning quickly, she scurried out of his kitchen. He could hear her taking the stairs up to her room. Max wanted to follow her up there. He wanted to make her his. He was never a playboy like Gutter Mouth or Foster, but he'd had his fair share of feminine company over the years. He never had a problem telling a woman what he wanted, so why the hell couldn't he make himself walk up those stairs? Perhaps because this time he wanted more than a casual hookup. This time he wanted it all.

Chapter Twelve

Max

Dinner with Foster and Mirabella helped create a buffer between him and Sloane. No matter the topic, he couldn't stop thinking of her kiss back in the hospital room. It was different from the one he'd given her at her apartment door that first night they met. It was passionate and promising. If they hadn't been interrupted, who knows where it could have led? He watched her talking to Bella. She was laughing and making motions with her hands. He'd never seen her so happy.

Every so often she would push her hair out of her eyes. Always with the hair—why she didn't just cut it, he couldn't figure out. Then again, the simple movement was sexy as hell. Max wondered what it would take for her to flirt with him the way she did with Kasper. Then he remembered the first time he met Brody. He said he always had to initiate everything. Could that mean even flirting? Kasper definitely didn't hold back on flirting with anyone.

Only one way to find out.

Max retrieved the bottle of wine from the kitchen. Leaning closer than he normally would, he topped off Sloane's glass. He tried to keep the smile off his face when she startled. Bowing down further, he placed his nose so close to her neck it was almost touching. He breathed her in.

"You smell amazing."

"Oh. Thank you." Her cheeks flushed slightly. That was a good sign, right?

"You're welcome. So, Bella, you getting cold feet yet?" he teased.

"Not even a little bit, Max." She grinned while wrapping her arm around one of Foster's.

"Don't give her any ideas." Foster shook his head playfully. "I'll never find another one even close to her if she smartens up now."

Everyone laughed, enjoying the tension-free evening. Max sat back down, winking at Sloane when she looked over at him. Her face twisted in confusion. Not the response he had been hoping for. She looked guarded. He wanted her smiling again.

"Sloane, you wanna help me with dessert?" Bella asked. "I got one of those incredible cheesecakes from that little bakery on the corner of Fifth and Salem Ave."

"Are you serious? Where is it?" Sloane jumped up from her seat and followed Bella, the sound of their laughter fading as they entered the kitchen.

Foster braced his arms on the table and leaned forward. His expression was warm, but muted. "You wanna talk about it?"

Max grimaced; he knew Foster wouldn't leave it

alone. Hell, at this point, maybe he had a few suggestions. He'd known Sloane for a while now.

"I don't know, man. I can't stop thinking about her. The kiss she laid on me at the hospital was amazing. Fucking Kasper keeps coming around and she shamelessly flirts with him right in front of me." Max dragged his hands through his thick hair. "I flirt with her and she looks at me like I've grown horns and started speaking in tongues."

"Let me start by asking you a very important question, Max."

"What?"

Foster raised his eyebrows. "Is the reason you want her because Kasper set his sights on her too?"

"What? No."

"Just asking. You're my best friend, but she's gonna be family. She doesn't have anyone else to look out for her."

"How could you ask me that? You know I'm not *that* guy. I've wanted her since the first time we met in your doorway, the night we had dinner. She was still seeing Brody then."

"Well, you were about to hook up with Charlie again until you saw her with Gutter Mouth. It was a reasonable question. I can't risk her getting hurt again. She met Brody because of me. If another one of my buddies fucks her over, neither one of those amazing women will forgive me anytime soon."

"I get it. I was only hooking up with Charlie to get Sloane off my damn mind. I'm so screwed." Foster was still laughing as the girls came back, each with two plates of cheesecake.

***

Sloane

"Soooo…are you gonna tell me about that steamy kiss we walked in on last night?"

"Keep it down," she whispered. The last thing Sloane needed was the guys overhearing their conversation.

"Oh don't you worry none. I'm sure Foster is asking the same thing. Now spill it."

Sloane took a deep breath and told Bella all about the powerful moment she'd shared with Max on the dance floor at The Void, the need to get away from him the next morning, and the slut nurse. Bella sat at the breakfast bar listening intensely until she finished up with how the kiss was nothing to him and the way he behaved when Kasper came by.

"Wow. He must have it bad." She giggled.

"Kasper doesn't seem like the type of man to get attached to a woman."

"I meant Max." Bella laughed again.

"Max? How did you come to that conclusion?" Sloane wished Bella were right, but she couldn't believe it could be true.

"I just know. It's like a page out of the 'Male Caveman 101' handbook. If he clubs you over the head and drags you off, remember, that's a good thing. Let's get back before they send a search party." They laughed all the way back to the table.

Sloane set one of the plates she carried in front of Max. He looked up smiling. His hand circled around her wrist as she straightened up, catching her off guard.

"Thank you." Max practically leveled her with his panty-dropping smile. Her thighs clamped together, trying to stop the sudden gush of liquid heat that magically appeared. Damn that man.

"You…You're welcome." Sloane knew she was blushing. She felt her body's betrayal heat her cheeks. *Great.* She sat down, lifting a fork full of cheesecake to her mouth. The moment the smooth chocolate-drizzled yumminess hit her tongue, she moaned in delight. "OhmyGod," she mumbled while chewing.

"Fantastic, isn't it?" Bella gushed from her seat.

"Mmmmm." Sloane licked the chocolate sauce from the fork before taking another bite.

Foster laughed. "Um, are you all right?"

"Oh wow. It's better than sex," she blurted between bites. She grimaced. *Shit!* Sloane hadn't meant to say that out loud.

Max chuckled. "Then you haven't been doing it right."

Her face heated. If you could die from humiliation, she would now be dead as a doornail. Maybe if she laughed they would think she'd just been joking. Except Bella—she knew the truth about her sad, practically nonexistent sex life. Sloane opened her eyes, and the laugh died on her lips from the intense look in Max's eyes. The air in the room felt thick and charged with a sexual tension that hadn't been there a few minutes ago. She wondered if she was imagining something where nothing was, yet again.

"Well, we had a great time, but we better get

going," Bella announced as she collected the plates. Sloane sat frozen, her eyes never leaving Max's. She was startled by Bella's arms wrapping around her shoulders. Sloane stood to hug her properly. She could hear Max and Foster saying their goodbyes as well.

"Thank you for bringing dinner. It was wonderful. Once I get my life back, I owe you guys dinner. Lots of dinners."

"That's what family is for, sweetie. Stay safe. I'll call you tomorrow. I love you."

"I love you, Bella."

"My turn." Foster embraced her in a bear hug. "You scared us, Robertson. Cut that shit out."

"Love you too," she answered sarcastically, even though she truly did love him for being worried about her. Bella hit the boyfriend lotto. Sloane was honored to call him family.

"Yeah, yeah. Love you too." He grinned.

Then they left her alone with Max. He was acting strange. She couldn't get a bead on him tonight. But that wasn't anything new, really. She couldn't understand him on a good day, no matter how hard she tried. She drained the rest of her wine before rinsing the glass and placing it into the dishwasher. Turning, she slammed into Max's body. She put her hands on his chest to steady herself.

"Sorry, Max. I didn't know you were there."

Max placed his hand on the one she had covering his heart. He slipped his other into her hair like he did while they were dancing. Her panties were already wet and he hadn't even done anything yet.

His lips softly covered hers. Slanting his head more, his tongue searched for admittance. Sloane opened for him, caressing his tongue with her own. She gripped his head, pulling him against her tighter. The warmth of his hand enveloped one of her breasts, rubbing gently until her nipple peaked into a tight pebble. She moaned her consent into his talented mouth. She wanted this. She needed this. She needed him.

Sloane let her hands explore his upper body. Gliding over his corded shoulders, back, and chest before returning to the nape of his neck. Max left one breast hard and achy in favor of the other. Both of his hands slid over and under her ass, pulling her into him. He lifted her in the air with ease. Her legs automatically wrapped around his waist, locking her ankles behind him.

Her back was suddenly up against the kitchen wall. Now that Max didn't have to support her full weight, he let his hands glide up her thighs. His calloused fingers snuck under the hem of her shirt. He finally broke the kiss to pull the shirt over her head, exposing the blue lace bra she wore. She grimaced slightly from the pain in her shoulder.

She felt heat blossom across her face and neck. Max dragged his gaze over her torso, and then lifted it to look at her. Hunger was reflected in his eyes. A lopsided grin slowly spread across his kiss-swollen lips. It was wicked, in the best way. A fresh gush of juices drenched her panties from that grin alone. All of the discomfort from her gunshot wound was forgotten. Nothing existed beyond this moment with Max. Without breaking eye contact, Max lowered his head, taking a nipple into his mouth. The lace of the bra lent a scratchy sensation completely at odds with the heat of his mouth. She yelped as his teeth made purchase on the swollen nub, but arched her back into him anyway. Hoping he would take more of her.

She slipped a hand between them, sneaking it under the waistband of his jeans. Her fingers grazed over his erection. The silky skin was warm. The tip oozed his arousal. He was so thick she could barely wrap her fingers all the way around him. She began stroking him. It was awkward with his pants still zipped, but now that she had him, she didn't want this moment to end. Max lifted his head and kissed her again, and their tongues matched the rhythm of her hand. Max moaned into her mouth. It was the sexiest thing she had ever heard.

She was hotter than she had ever been for a man in her entire life. It felt like her skin was on fire. Her breath was ragged and all she was doing was gripping him with her hand. If they had sex—and at this rate, she hoped to God that they would—she wasn't sure she could come back from something like this. This could break her. The intensity was so much more than she could have ever imagined sharing with someone.

Max turned on his heel and perched her ass on the edge of his kitchen island. Then, his fingers went to work on her jeans. With the offending fabric unbuttoned and unzipped, he grabbed both sides, yanking them down along with her panties that perfectly matched her bra. Both articles were wet in the center.

131

"Wow," Max breathed across her bare mound. The moment his mouth latched onto her clit, sucking it between his lips, she gasped with pleasure. He began tracing up her thighs with his tongue. He licked up one until he met her weeping lips, then he repeated the motions with the other. Tasting every inch of her. Methodically driving her absolutely crazy.

He felt amazing—she couldn't get enough of him. Sloane rocked her hips forward until he finally plunged his tongue inside. She grabbed a fist full of his hair. The man worked her body like a concert violinist. Plucking and stroking. Flicking his tongue across her swollen clit as he slid first one, then two fingers inside of her. Her imminent orgasm built rapidly. "Oh God, Max. Please!" she begged.

Max increased his speed, sucking harder. Her body began to tremble uncontrollably. Her arms, braced on the counter behind her, kept trying to give out. She struggled to stay upright. Max stopped long enough to push her onto her back and toss both of her legs over his shoulders. With her body suspended so she wouldn't fall, Max went back to his ministrations, his eyes never leaving her face. It only took seconds for the wave of pleasure to overcome her. She came, screaming almost violently. He continued to lap up her juices as the most mind-blowing orgasm of her life came to an end.

Straightening to his full height, Max pulled her into his arms, kissing her hard. She could taste herself on his lips. Instead of turning her off, as it had the only time Brody had taken the time to do it, with Max, it only renewed her arousal. Then again, Brody hadn't given her an orgasm, amazing or otherwise. She wanted to make Max feel as good as he'd made her. She just didn't know how. No, she knew what she wanted to do. Except the one and only time she'd tried, it was a disaster. Still, she wanted to try. She craved the taste of him.

***

Max

Max couldn't take his eyes off of Sloane. Her head was thrown back with pure ecstasy written across her beautiful face. It had to be the most amazing thing he had ever witnessed. That was until she came screaming his name. He almost came in his pants like a horny teenager. Her cream gushed into his mouth. He lapped up every drop he could. Savoring her taste. He held her in his arms afterward and kissed her, all the while feeling like his heart would burst from his chest. She was perfect. He had to have her. All of her.

Sloane reached forward again, this time undoing his jeans. His erection sprang out as she lowered the denim off of his hips. Her breath hitched as she drank him in. He remembered all the things that bastard Brody said about her. That she was cold and vanilla. There was no way Max would use those words to describe her. He also recalled him saying he cheated because she wouldn't blow him. What a loser. To give up a passion like this over a blowjob was asinine. He'd had his fair share of BJ's over the

133

years and not all of them were good.

Then she did the one thing he never thought she would do. She pushed on his shoulders until he backed away, slid from the counter, and lowered herself to her knees. Her eyes searched his. What she was looking for, he wasn't sure. In her eyes, he felt as though he could see into her soul. The passion, the want, the need to please him. It was breathtaking. In that moment of vulnerability, he knew deep down that he was completely, head over heels in love with her.

Her soft lips pressed gently against the swollen tip of his cock. It jerked involuntarily. Taking that as a positive sign, her tongue darted out, swiping the bead of pre-cum off the slit. Swirling the flat of her tongue around him, she took the head completely into her mouth. The warm wet enclosure almost brought him to his knees. She began bobbing her head up and down his shaft slowly.

"Mmmm," he groaned.

Max fisted his hands at his sides. He knew he was above average in length and he didn't want to hurt her. Plus, this was her show. He wasn't about to take control away from her. He laced his fingers behind his head and watched her. Her hand gripped his base, stroking in time to her mouth. His cock was slick with her saliva. The first time she made slurping sounds, he almost blew then and there. He pulled her up off her knees.

"Did I do something wrong?" She looked so scared and hurt it almost broke his heart. Once again he wished he could beat Brody's face in.

"God, no. I don't know how much longer I can

last. I don't want the first time to be like this. I need to be inside you."

"Oh." Her smile lit up the room.

Max pulled up his pants enough so he could walk, leaving her clothes all over the kitchen. He threw Sloane over his shoulder in a fireman's carry. Hustling, he took the stairs two at a time. Finally, he laid her out onto his bed. He removed her bra, revealing her milky white breasts. The nipples were dark pink and still erect. Shedding his clothing as quickly as possible, he climbed onto the bed with her. Her thighs cradled his hips perfectly. He pressed his hard, naked body into her soft one. Kissing her softly, he pressed his forehead to hers.

"I need you," he whispered in the dark.

"Take me, Max. Please."

"I don't know how long I can last with you."

"We have all night." The smile on her sweet lips was stunning.

Max rubbed his cock back and forth against her lips, lubricating himself. He pushed his hips forward, sinking into her soft flesh. Her pussy was warm and tight. He had to work to get himself all the way in. He didn't want to hurt her. He never wanted to hurt her, so he went slowly. Once he was seated inside her as far as he could go, Max let her body adjust for a moment. When he couldn't take it anymore, he began moving. Sliding in and out of her slick heat. The way her tight channel sucked him back in was astounding. The tingling started in his toes, spreading up his body to pool in his tight balls.

"Shit baby, I can't hold it much longer."

"Don't hold back, Max. Come with me. Oh God, Max. Max, I'm coming." She screamed.

Sloane's nails dug into his ass cheeks as she held on, grinding her hips up to meet his. Max continued to pump into her, his thrusts intensifying in speed and strength. She came undone underneath him, washing his cock in her cream. With one more thrust, he emptied himself inside her. Spurt after spurt coated her walls. He came longer and harder than he could remember ever doing before. Rolling over so she was on top, Max held her until their breathing returned to normal.

"That was amazing, Max."

"That's an understatement." He chuckled.

"I don't think that could be topped."

"Give me ten minutes."

They both laughed. Max rubbed his hands up and down her bare skin. Even slick with sweat and her hair matted to her face, she was beautiful. Beautiful and his. His cock started to stiffen inside her.

"Already?" She giggled, sounding surprised. Hell, so was he. Usually he was a one and done for the night. With Sloane, he couldn't get enough of her. She sat up, straddling his hips. Rocking back and forth, she preceded to ride him. Eventually Max flipped her over, covering her body, claiming her. For the first time, Max made love to a woman with his body, mind, and soul.

It was something he would never forget.

Chapter Thirteen

Max

Max woke to the sound of his phone buzzing against the side of the dresser. He was still wrapped around Sloane's sleeping body. He hated to move away from her, but he didn't want the buzzing to wake her either. Reluctantly he got up, searching his pockets for the annoying thing. Gutter Mouth flashed across the screen. He accepted the call, taking one last look at her angelic face before he left the bedroom as quietly as he could.

"Yeah."

"Hey, man. Thought I'd give you a heads up. Petrov's boy, Booker, was spotted two blocks from Sloane's apartment. By the time the cops got there he was long gone. I have some more leads coming in; hopefully I'll be able to get a bead on him soon."

"Thanks, Gutter Mouth."

"Sure, I don't want to see anything happen to Sloane either, man. There's something about that girl."

"That there is." Max smiled, thinking about the way she looked when she climaxed above him last night.

"Are you interested?"

"Only a fool wouldn't be. I'm more than interested." He didn't want to tell his buddy about last night. He wanted that to stay between him and Sloane.

"What about that chick you were with the other night?"

"Charlie," Max sighed. "It was a mistake. One I don't intend to make again."

"So she wasn't your girlfriend? Because she sure as shit acted like it."

"Hell no, she isn't my girlfriend. I needed a release, she was willing. End of story. Except I couldn't do it. Fuck, man. I know it sounds crazy, but you're right about Sloane. She's special. No matter what I've tried to tell myself, I know, without a doubt, that I'm in love with her."

There was a moment of silence, then Gutter Mouth let out a loud whistle.

"Damn, Max. I never thought I'd see the day."

"Shut the fuck up," Max half joked.

"I get it. I do. Know one thing, though. If you ever fuck up, I won't hesitate to make her mine."

"Over my dead body."

Kasper laughed. "If that's what it takes...I better go, I'm waitin' for Mother to call me back about Booker. I'll hit you up later. Give Sloane sloppy kisses from me." He laughed before hanging up.

***

Sloane

Sloane woke up to an empty bed. Every muscle in her body was sore in the most delicious way. Except for her shoulder. *That* pain was real and intense. She wished Max would've still been here when she woke up. Spotting his t-shirt on the floor, she picked it up. Pressing it to her face, she breathed him in. She pulled it over her head before going downstairs to find him and some aspirin. She finger combed her hair on the way down the steps, trying to tame the mess. She paused in the kitchen at the sound of his voice. He was outside on the phone with someone. Just before she could walk away, she heard him whisper something that made her immediately stiffen.

"Charlie." Max rubbed his hand through his hair. "It was a mistake. One I don't intend to make again."

Oh my God. No, this couldn't be happening. Max made love to her all night long. He couldn't be on the phone confessing to Charlie that it was all a mistake. Sloane couldn't breathe. She was frozen in place.

"Hell no, she isn't my girlfriend. I needed a release, she was willing. End of story."

Pain ripped through her heart. She fell to her knees, and the cold tiles bit into her skin. She could hear his voice, but the words were completely lost to her now. She had heard enough already.

Unwanted sobs wracked her. Brody's betrayal hurt, but Max had successfully destroyed her. She gave him everything she had to give last night. Her

139

heart and soul were his and she was nothing more than a willing release for him. She thought he was different. She actually believed they had something special starting. She was a damn fool.

Pissed at herself for giving so completely, Sloane picked herself up off the floor. She felt used and dirty. She had to scrub him off her skin. Scrubbing him from her heart wasn't going to be nearly as easy, but she knew it had to be done. Sooner rather than later. She wouldn't waste years giving her love to a man who threw it back in her face. No. Never again. She couldn't bring herself to enter his room again, so her bra would have to stay where it was. Sloane sent Bella a text message.

Sloane: Need you now. Please hurry.

The water burned her sensitive skin. She scoured every inch of herself with a loofah. She knew her stitches were soaked through, but she couldn't bring herself to care about anything else. At least she remembered to take off the bandage before getting under the spray.

Her pale skin looked red and angry by the time she was done. She didn't care. Her skin could bleed and she'd still scrub him away. Dressing quickly in jeans and a t-shirt, she started filling her suitcase. She made sure she had all of her belongings, sans bra that still remained somewhere in his bedroom. She wasn't sure what she would say to him when they came face to face. The only thing she was certain of, was that she would *not* cry.

Sloane decided that she would pretend like

everything was fine. She would act like it was no big deal. Act like her world wasn't crushed. She would not let him see her broken. That's what she was, broken. She refused to run away again. This time she would make it clear that she was leaving and didn't need him to look after her. Max was pouring coffee into an oversized mug when she reached the kitchen.

"Good morning, beautiful." He grinned at her. If not for overhearing his conversation this morning with Charlie, Sloane would have melted then and there for him.

"Hey." She smiled back, knowing full well it didn't reach her eyes. Max retrieved another mug. He filled it before handing it off to her. "Thank you."

"So…" He crossed his ankles as he leaned back against the counter. His sexy smile never faltered. "What do you wanna do today?"

"Oh, I'm sorry. I already made plans for today. Bella should be here any minute."

"Sure, no problem. I just thought we would spend the day together."

"That's nice of you, but I know you're probably sick of being cooped up here with me. I'm going to go to the apartment today. I have to get it cleaned up. I'm not sure if I'm going to stay there anymore, but regardless I can't let the mess go any longer."

"You're leaving?" He sounded surprised.

Perhaps most women didn't want to walk away from him the next morning. Then again, they probably knew it was just sex and nothing more before they put their heart into it. If she meant half as much to him as he meant to her, she wouldn't want to leave either.

"I think it's time. We both knew this was temporary. I appreciate everything you did for me, Max."

"Sloane, it still isn't safe."

"We don't know how long it will take to find this guy. I can't hide out here forever."

Against her better judgment, Sloane walked toward him. She took his face in her hands. Looking into those beautiful eyes, she almost chickened out. She knew that if she fell into his arms again it would only hurt even more when he was the one to end things. She could feel the tears trying to pool in her eyes. She pressed her lips to his gently once, twice, before withdrawing to meet his gaze again.

"Thank you for everything, Max. I'll never forget what you've done for me."

They could hear Bella honk the horn outside. Sloane placed her hand on Max's cheek one last time before grabbing the handle to her suitcase. The wheels clicked on the tiles as she pulled it behind her. A tear escaped, rolling down her face as she descended the deck stairs. She could feel Max's eyes on her. She refused to look back. She had to get to Bella before he could see her fall apart. She threw the suitcase in the back seat. Taking her first deep breath since coming face to face with Max this morning, she sat in the passenger seat next to Bella.

"Drive."

With the house—and Max—in the rear view, she slumped in the seat, burying her face in her hands. She stopped trying to be brave. She didn't need to hold it together any longer. Bella was here with her. She would help Sloane through this. She knew she wasn't dying no matter what her shattered heart believed.

The car ride to her apartment was made in sweet silence. Her cousin would want to give Sloane her uninterrupted attention when she told her sad story—Bella wouldn't want the distraction of driving. That was just fine by Sloane.

Entering the apartment was surreal. Glass still littered the floor in various areas and there were black smudges all over where the police had dusted for fingerprints. She had a big cleanup job ahead of her. She welcomed the distraction. First things first, though.

"Sloane, honey, what happened?" Bella asked once they were safely locked away from the world.

"I thought he was different. I thought we had a connection. Oh Bella, I fell in love with him. I don't know what I was thinking."

"Everything seemed fine last night. Better even. Tell me what happened," she urged.

"We made love. Multiple times. Until we were both too exhausted to move. It was amazing. Earth shattering, mind blowing, like nothing I've ever experienced kind of amazing, Bella. I gave him everything. I held nothing back for the first time in…I can't even remember."

Sloane's tears continued streaming down her face. She couldn't stop them if she tried. She dropped to the floor in front of her couch. Bella lowered herself to sit next to her.

"That sounds incredible, Sloane. I knew you two

would be perfect together. So what's with the water works?"

"This morning I woke up alone. Even so, I was so happy. I put on his shirt and went to find him. He was outside on his phone, Bella. He was whispering like he didn't want to be overheard, but I heard him." Sloane hugged her knees to her chest, rocking back and forth. She was gasping for air trying to get the rest of the story out. Bella rubbed her back, waiting patiently. She knew Sloane would get there; she just needed a minute.

"I heard him say 'Charlie.'"

"Oh no!" Bella pulled Sloane into her arms. "Maybe he was—"

"No, Bella, don't make excuses. He told her I was a mistake. He told her I was nothing more than a willing participant for his release. I gave him my heart and I was nothing more than a warm body to him. I feel like a goddamn fool," she yelled. Her heart was breaking all over again as she recounted the story out loud.

"That can't be right, Sloane. I've seen the way he looks at you."

"I had to get out of there." Sloane ignored her comment. "I need to focus on putting my life back together. A new job, a new apartment, a new life, Bella. That's what I need, starting right now."

"Well then, let's start getting this place packed up and make some calls."

Chapter Fourteen

Max

It had been over a month since Sloane walked out of Max's life. She moved from her apartment and changed her cell phone number. He didn't know what had happened. Why did she walk out on him? They had just started something incredible. He felt her absence every day.

Foster and Gutter Mouth would only confirm that she was all right. The few times he saw Bella, she scowled at him before leaving the room. That was something she had never done before.

What the hell? Did he do something wrong with Sloane? He replayed the last 24 hours they spent together over in his mind for the hundredth time. He couldn't think of one thing except letting her leave. Why did he let her go? After the third day with no word from her, he knew it was over. His heart ached for her. He had never loved anyone before, and he never would again.

He tried not to think about his heartache as he

entered his mother's living room.

"Hey, Ma." He wrapped his tiny mother in his arms. She was small and fragile.

Her thin eyebrows pinched together as she pulled away from him. "What is it, Max?"

"It's nothing, Ma."

"Don't lie to me, boy. I'm your mother; I know when something is eating you. You look like you're being devoured from the inside out, right now."

Max sighed, scrubbing a hand over his face. "I met a girl—it ended before it could really begin, and I don't know why. It's got me mixed up inside."

His mother looked surprised. "A girl?"

"Yeah."

His mom smiled at him. "Is she pretty?"

"Beautiful, but didn't you hear me? It's over."

Her expression sobered. "Why?"

He shook his head in defeat. "I don't know."

"I've never seen you like this over a girl, Max. Do you love her?"

"Yeah, Ma, I do. I love her." A wide grin stretched across her face. "Why are you smiling?" Max asked suspiciously.

"It's not like you to give up anything without a fight."

"She moved and changed her number. What am I supposed to do?"

Now the crazed woman was belly laughing at him. His own mother. She actually had tears in her eyes, she was laughing so hard.

"What the hell, Ma?" Max was getting pissed. He came here for a little comfort, not to have his pain laughed at. Especially not by her.

"Oh honey, I'm sorry, but you're a private investigator for crying out loud. It's your job to find people that don't want to be found. What are you waiting for?"

"I don't know what I did to make her leave in the first place. Until I can figure that out, how can I fix us?"

"All's fair in love and war. Play dirty. Don't give this girl up without fighting for her, Max. You'll never forgive yourself. You'll always wonder 'What if' and that's no way to live. Understand me?"

Fight dirty, she says. Yeah, he could do that. Max knew just where to start too. With his resolve in place, he kissed her forehead. "I understand. I've gotta go, Ma. I have an idea."

"That's my boy. Now go get that girl back. I wanna meet the woman that stole my baby's heart."

After leaving his mom, Max drove straight to Foster's house. He was getting some answers this time. He walked with confidence up to the front door. Bella answered after the second knock.

"Max. What are you doing here? Foster is at work."

"I know. I came to talk to you."

"Me? Why me?"

Without waiting for an invitation, Max entered the house just like he had dozens of times in the past. She looked nervous and yet defiant at the same time. She was so cute; it was no wonder Foster was smitten. The wedding was rapidly approaching. Max didn't want to face Sloane for the first time since she left at the rehearsal dinner in front of everyone.

"Please, Mirabella. I know she talked to you. I don't know what I did, but I can't keep on like this," he roared. "She just walked away like it didn't mean a damn thing. I've waited weeks for her to tell me what went wrong. I need to know. That woman drives me crazy, but I can't stop loving her any more that I can stop breathing."

Max raked his hands through his hair. He didn't mean to yell at her, but he couldn't help himself. A tear slid down his cheek when he raised his head to meet her eyes. She looked shocked. Why did everyone think it was so unheard of for him to feel something for someone? Sure, he never had before, but that's because he didn't know Sloane before. She was everything he never knew he'd wanted.

"I'm sorry, did you say *love*?"

"Yeah, I did."

"Whoa. Stop right there and let's take this step-by-step. When did you fall in love with my cousin?" Bella put her hands on her hips and waited for him to answer.

"When? I don't know, exactly. I knew I wanted her the moment I saw her. I knew for sure, without a fuckin' doubt, before I took her to my bed though. I don't know if Foster ever mentioned it, but I don't bring women to my house. There are definitely no overnight guests, ever."

"Why is that?" She sounded sincerely intrigued.

"Someday when I settle down, I don't want my girl to have to wonder how many women were in my bed, or if I took them on the couch or kitchen floor. I wanted every experience to be new and special."

"Then why, Max? Why did you pick Sloane?" Tears were freely flowing from Bella now.

"Because I love her."

"No, Max. Why did you tell Charlie that Sloane was a mistake, that she was just a release to you?" she yelled at him.

"What the hell are you talking about? I haven't talked to Charlie since she left the club that night with you guys."

"The next morning Sloane heard you on the deck. You were whispering on the phone with her."

"I was talking to Gutter Mouth. To answer the other question, I wasn't talking about Sloane, I was talking about *Charlie*. Gutter Mouth has the hots for Sloane. I told him Charlie meant nothing, that I was in love with Sloane."

Max stood up and paced back and forth. He couldn't believe it. After what they shared that night, she actually believed he felt nothing for her. Was she blind?

"Call him and ask him if you don't believe me, Bella. I need her. Please help me."

***

Sloane

Sloane had been in her new apartment on the opposite end of town for a few weeks. She had been working ridiculous hours as a waitress at Sully's, a trendy bar and grill. It was tiring being on her feet all the time, but it kept her mind busy. The less time she had to think about Max, the better off she would be.

She had thought time would make the memories bittersweet, but time didn't always heal. Every day she missed him more. She had to stop herself from wondering what he was doing. Or who he was doing. Her heart couldn't take the answer.

Tonight would be a madhouse. A huge fight was playing on the television screens. She didn't know the names of the guys beating each other's face in; however, she knew her tips would be improved because of them. The crowds were already filling in. Normally she welcomed the chaos, but this damn flu was kicking her ass this last week.

"Hottie alert at your table seven, Sloane." Donna grinned as she walked past.

"Great," she mumbled. The other girls got excited when good-looking guys sat in their areas and flirted with them. Slone only compared them all to Max. Every one of them she found wanting. A lone man sat at table seven. With the menu concealing his face, she began her rehearsed speech to get his attention.

"Good evening. My name's Sloane. I'll be your waitress tonight. Can I get you something to drink to start with?"

The man slowly lowered his menu. Staring back at her were the same whiskey eyes that haunted her dreams each and every night. She was stunned.

"Max?" she barely whispered.

"Yes, you can start by sitting down and talking with me," he said smugly. Bastard.

"I'm working, Max. What do you want?"

Sloane was getting impatient as he sat there smiling. What was he doing here? How had he found out where she worked? Did he just happen to come in here today for dinner by chance? Was he meeting a date here? That last thought soured her stomach.

"We need to talk, Sloane. Now. I'm not waiting anymore. I've given you more than a month. That's all you're getting."

"I'm not doing this."

Sloane turned to walk away. Donna could take his table. She would most likely be in his lap with her tongue down his throat before last call. That's what usually happened on Fridays and Saturdays with her. The thought made Sloane's stomach churn even more than some random date showing up...He didn't want her, but she still loved him.

She couldn't sit and watch him with someone new, especially not someone Sloane worked with. She felt the bile rising. Max grabbed her arm, spinning her quickly to face him. Too quickly. The whole world spun along with her. The burning sensation filled her mouth at the same time as her saliva glands decided to work triple time. She threw up on the floor in front of them.

"Sloane, baby. Are you okay?" His voice was laced with concern. He held on to both of her upper arms as she tried to get the room to stop spinning. Maybe she was sicker than she originally thought. The spinning wasn't slowing down. If anything, it was speeding up. Before she could answer him, everything went black.

Sloane woke up in another hospital bed. This

was becoming a bad habit. She had an IV needle in her hand with clear fluids running into it from the bag hanging by the bed. She didn't feel any shittier than before, so that must be a good sign. Actually, she *did* feel a little better. She breathed a sigh of relief.

A gentle knock sounded at the door before a doctor entered the small room. He looked up from his clipboard. His smile was almost as sexy as Max's, and his brown eyes were so dark they almost looked black. His brown hair was a little longer than she would have expected from a doctor, and the tips were dyed blond. He looked so much like an actor playing a doctor on a cable show that she scanned the room for cameras.

"Ms. Robertson, it's good to see you awake. I'm Dr. Hutchinson, but most of my patients call me Dr. Hank." He extended his hand for her to shake.

"Is everything all right? I feel a lot better now." Okay, so she was stretching the truth a bit, but he couldn't know that.

"How long have you been feeling sick?"

"I've been kinda tired the last two weeks or so, but this last week has been brutal. I'll be glad when this damn flu is gone." She let her head fall back into the pillow. A moment later she lifted her head back up. "Um, did anyone come here with me?"

Sloane had been both hoping and dreading that Max would be there when she woke up. She knew they couldn't be together, but damn, she wanted to see him again even though she knew it would just make things harder for her in the long run.

"There was a gentleman here with you. Last I

saw, he was in the waiting room on the phone. So let's just jump right on in, shall we?" He smiled. "Are you married?"

"No."

"Are you seeing someone?"

"Um, no. What does my relationship status have to do with why I'm he—" Her eyes widened. "OH MY GOD!" Sloane yelled, jumping up to a sitting position, the IV tugging painfully on her hand. "Did that rat bastard give me an STD?"

Dr. Hank had the audacity to burst out in a full-out belly laugh. Sloane didn't see the humor in finding out she'd gotten a venereal disease. *Please let it be treatable.* She was gonna kill him. She was gonna cut his—

"Goodness no, Ms. Robertson."

"Sloane, just call me Sloane."

"I asked because well, Sloane, you're pregnant."

Pregnant. She just stared at him. She could feel her mouth hanging open. She wanted to close it. She just couldn't seem to manage to make anything move at the moment. Pregnant, oh God. How did this happen? ...Never mind, she knew how it happened. She remembered every delicious moment of how it happened.

What was she going to do? How was she going to raise a child on her own? No, she couldn't think that way. Bella would be there to help her. Plus, her parents would support her any way she needed. Shit, she was going to have a baby. She was going to have *Max's* baby.

"I take it from your expression and from my earlier questions, that this was an unplanned pregnancy?"

"It was an unplanned affair. Not even an affair, it was one night with a friend that meant more to me than him. Shit," she blurted out.

"Well, we're going to need a follow-up appointment to get a family history, and at that time we can do a sonogram to find out how far along you are."

"About four weeks," she mumbled.

Another knock on the door. Sloane looked up at it, waiting for a nurse to walk in, but no one did. Dr. Hank answered when she didn't.

"Come in."

Max opened the door, and she wanted to crawl in a hole. He looked like it had been a while since his face saw a razor. She knew exactly what it felt like to have his stubble brush against her sensitive skin.

"How is she, Doc?"

"Flu," she blurted. "Just the flu. I'll be fine. Thank you, doctor. I'll be sure to call your office later today to set up a follow-up appointment. Thank you for everything." He gave Sloane a mischievous smile. Her guess was that he'd just realized Max was this baby's father.

"Take care of yourself, Sloane. Get plenty of rest and double your fluid intake. You were severely dehydrated when you came in. It's no wonder you fainted." He pulled a small business card from the front pocket of his white coat. "Here's my card." Before handing it to her, he flipped it over on his clipboard and wrote something on the back. "My cell phone number is on the back. If you need anything, call me."

"Thank you," she replied while taking the offered card. "When can I leave?"

"I'll start your discharge papers now."

He stood up and made his way to the door. He gave a chin nod to Max before leaving them alone. Alone again with Max. That's how she'd ended up in this mess. She looked over at him. He stood there with his hands in his front pockets, his gaze locked on hers. His stare was so intense that she wanted to pull the covers over her head and hide until he left. Why the hell did he have to look so good?

"Are you really okay?"

"Yes, Max, I'm fine."

"I called Foster. He said he would get Bella and meet us at your place."

"Thank you. You don't have to take me home. I can get a ride."

Max stalked over to her and planted both of his hands on the arm rail of the bed. Sloane could see his knuckles turning white with the force of his grip. He looked angry as hell and the fact that it was directed toward her was terrifying. She knew he wouldn't hurt her physically, but it didn't stop her from leaning back into her pillow further.

"Why the hell would I leave you on your own to get home when, one, I wanted to talk to you in the first place. Two, you're obviously sick and need some help. Now let's get you outta here."

Once Sloane hopped up into Max's truck, she gave him directions to her new apartment. So much for him not knowing where she lived anymore. Then again, if he'd found her at work, he could find her at home.

155

He parked his truck in the underground garage in one of her assigned parking spots since her car was still at Sully's. Sloane's guest spot was currently occupied by a silver Ford Focus belonging to Bella. Since she wasn't inside of it, Sloane knew she must already be upstairs in her apartment. She was the only person Sloane trusted with her spare key.

The elevator ride was silent. She didn't know what to say to Max. Surprisingly he hadn't said anything to her either. Being this close to him again was wreaking havoc with her sensibilities. Part of her wanted to scream at him. The other part wanted to rub herself up against him and purr. She had to get him to leave so she could talk to Bella.

"You better not be sick for my wedding," Bella yelled, getting up from the couch.

"I'll be fine by then," Sloane lied.

"Good thing." She smiled. "Foster ran to pick up some essentials. You hardly have anything in your pantry. When's the last time you went grocery shopping? Never mind, it's not important. He should be back any minute, so let's get you settled."

"Thanks for the ride, Max," Sloane called over her shoulder as she walked toward the bedroom.

"I'm not leaving, Sloane," he replied firmly while he shook his head in amusement. "I need to talk to Foster, I might as well wait here for him."

Sloane didn't say anything else to him. She just continued on to her bedroom with Bella close behind. Once they were inside, she plopped down on the bed, falling backward. Bella shut the door quietly behind her.

"Maybe you should talk with him, Sloane."

"I can't. Please, Bella. You don't understand what I'm going through right now."

"I know you're sick, honey. I just think he—"

"Damn it, Bella, I don't want to talk about it."

"All right. We won't talk about it." She took a step back. Sloane knew she'd hurt Bella's feelings, but she was still processing her own right now.

"Get some sleep. I'll bring you some soup in a little bit."

"I'm sorry, Bella."

"I understand. No worries."

Sloane stripped out of her clothes. Pulling a t-shirt on, she snuggled under the covers. It didn't take long before she was sound asleep.

***

Max

Max sat on the couch with his head in his hands. Hearing a door creak open, he looked up in time to see Bella emerge from Sloane's bedroom. She looked tired and upset. Max stood up and pulled her into a hug.

"She's gonna be fine."

"I was so worried when you called, Max. She hasn't been herself. I know she's going to be all right eventually, but I miss her."

"She won't talk to me. I don't know what to do."

"Just give her a little time. That's what we've all been doing. I'll try to put in a good word for you."

"Thanks."

It wasn't long before Foster came through the

door struggling not to drop all the bags he was carrying. Max rushed over to grab a few from him.

"Let me help, man."

"She hasn't thrown you out yet, that's a good sign." Foster smiled.

"She's asleep."

"Ah, okay."

Max helped Foster take everything out of the shopping bags and place it on the countertop. Bella put the things in their proper places.

"How long has she been sick?" he asked.

"She first told me she felt under the weather last week. I didn't realize she was this bad, though. It's probably all the hours she's putting in at that sports bar."

"Why isn't she working in an office somewhere? That's what she did before."

"She said she needed the money while she waited on interviews."

Max frowned. "Do you mind if I stick around? I really need to talk to her."

"Of course you can. I can't guarantee she'll talk to you, though."

Bella patted his shoulder before leaving the kitchen for Sloane's room. This time she carried with her a tray covered in food. Max took a moment to nose around the apartment. It was smaller than her last place and the neighborhood wasn't quite as good, but it wasn't bad either. He recognized the same furniture. Figuring he might as well get comfortable, Max once again took a seat on the couch, leaning his head back to rest.

Max woke up to the sound of a door opening. It

was dark out now and he didn't see Bella or Foster. How long had he slept? Stretching his back, he watched Sloane walk into the kitchen. He got up slowly, entering the room behind her. He missed the sight of her in those little cotton shorts. Hell, he just missed the sight of her.

"How are you feeling?"

"Better. I'm surprised you're still here."

"Why?" he asked, confused. She knew he wanted to talk to her.

"Just am." She shrugged her shoulders. There was a sadness about her that he hadn't seen before. He had to see her smile.

"Sloane…"

"I'd really rather not discuss it, Max." She stood next to the kitchen sink, looking down the drain. She couldn't even look at him.

"Well, we are going to discuss it. You can't just walk out on me without an explanation. As to what you think you heard that morning, you were dead fucking wrong."

***

Sloane

Max stood there with his arms folded across his chest. God, why did he always have to look so good? His hair had grown out a little more on top. His five o'clock shadow was sexy as hell. Mentioning that night stirred something inside her involuntarily. Her mind played back delicious moments that she knew she would cherish for all of

159

her days. The reminder of that one perfect night was growing in her belly…Wait. What did he just say? How did he know what she'd heard him say?

"What?" she stammered.

"You know what I'm talking about."

"It doesn't matter now."

Slapping his hand on the counter, Max bellowed, "The hell it doesn't!"

"I'm seeing someone, Max. Whatever happened between us, it just doesn't matter."

Sloane hated to lie to him. It broke her heart all over again to see the look that blanketed his handsome face. Immediately she wanted to take the words back. She should tell him she was lying. Only how could she tell him that night was the best night of her life? She knew what she heard. Knowing Charlie was on his mind was enough. It told her all she needed to know. She was just one more in what she was sure was a long line of discarded women.

The reality of it was, it wasn't just her anymore. Sloane was carrying his child. She wasn't going to be an obligation. The next man she made love to would want her for who she was. Since she was pregnant, that was a problem for the far-off future.

"Oh, I see. That was quick."

Max stalked over to where she stood. Her blood started rushing through her body, as her heart sped up. Why could this man do this to her? Did he see through her lie? He took her face into his hands, looking into her eyes. For the briefest of moments, Sloane thought he would kiss her like he did when they'd made love. She had butterflies from the anticipation.

"I guess it meant more to me, than it did to you."

He released her face slowly. Reality hit her like a sledgehammer to the solar plexus. He believed her. He walked to the front door, giving one last look over his shoulder, and then he walked out. Without another word. She sent away the man she loved. Sloane sat down on the cold vinyl floor and cried. What woman in their right mind would send away the man she loved? The kind that knew she could never keep him.

Eventually, she picked herself up. She needed to figure out what she was going to do. She had a lot of planning to do. Thank goodness Bella's wedding was sooner rather than later. No way could she hide her lie much longer.

Chapter Fifteen

Sloane

It was the day of Bella and Foster's wedding. Sloane woke up feeling as if she had been run over by a truck. Twice. Unfortunately, she didn't have the luxury of looking that way. She knew she had to put on her big girl panties and her best smile. Pulling her long hair up into a messy bun, Sloane put her makeup and other toiletries into an overnight bag to take with her to Bella's house. They would be getting ready there before heading to the church.

Sloane let herself into Bella's house carrying the bag over her shoulder. Bella was upstairs and Sloane could hear music playing in her room. The look of pure happiness on her face when Bella spotted her in the mirror instantly warmed Sloane's heart. She didn't have on any makeup and her hair was pulled back in a ponytail, but in that moment, Sloane had never seen her look more beautiful. Foster was a lucky man. The best part was, he knew it.

"You're late, but I forgive you." Bella got up from her vanity chair to wrap her arms around her.

"Only by five minutes."

"Sloane, I love you. Thank you for being a part of today."

"You're family and my best friend. Wild horses couldn't keep me away."

"Okay, let's get this party started."

Bella had all the rollers in Sloane's hair before her stylist, Fern, arrived. This cut down on the time Fern needed to work on her. While Sloane worked on her own makeup, Fern set about the task of piling Bella's hair on the top of her head so her veil would encompass an elegant bun. Inside the bun, rhinestones sparkled when she moved.

With her hair done, Bella moved on to her makeup as Fern removed Sloane's rollers. She gathered all the hair into a beautiful mass of curls at the base of her neck. Her unruly bangs were tamed with styling gel. It almost felt unnatural to not have to push them out of her eyes. All Sloane had left to do was put on the bridesmaid gown. She had to hand it to Bella—she picked out a dress that would flatter her, not make her look like a walking stick of cotton candy.

The black chiffon maxi dress fit her frame perfectly. The A-line hid the few pounds she had gained since she got pregnant. No one would be able to tell. Since she had to stand across from Max through the entire ceremony, she was doubly grateful for it. Sloane smoothed her fingertips over the silk of the bodice. Standing in front of the full-length mirror, she looked for any other telltale signs that she had a life growing inside of her. Nope, it was still her secret for now.

Sloane helped Bella into her gown. It was a beautiful fitted ivory dress with delicate embroidered tulle in a rose motif. The dress was everything that Bella was herself. She looked elegant and ethereal standing there ready to promise herself forever to the man who completed her. Sloane's heart was full of happiness for her, but she would be lying to herself if she said she didn't feel a twinge of sadness for her own love life. Or lack thereof. Today was not going to be an easy day. Not only would she see Max, but being as he was Foster's partner, she knew Brody would be there as well.

"You're absolutely stunning. Foster isn't going to be able to keep his eyes or hands off of you." Sloane laughed.

"I hope not; I fully intend to start our family tonight." She waggled her eyebrows with a huge grin on her face.

They joked and giggled their way outside to the black town car that waited for them. Since the wedding was kept small and intimate, Bella wanted everyone else to meet at the church. She didn't want all the women fussing with her or giving advice. She wanted it to be just the two of them. Like it always was. Sloane knew their parents—no, make that their moms—were less than thrilled. They wanted to be there, of course, but Bella wouldn't budge. She stood firm on what she'd wanted. In the end the women backed off. As the car pulled away from the curb, Sloane took a deep breath. Here goes nothing.

***

Max

Max and Foster stood side by side in their tuxedos smiling for the camera. Foster's father, Ren, lowered the camera with a huge grin on his face.

"You boys are looking good."

"Thanks, Dad."

"Are you ready for this?"

"More than ready, I know she's the one."

"I'm happy for you, son."

Ren pulled Foster into his embrace as Max stood by watching. Bella really was the perfect girl for Foster. Max couldn't be happier for him. He just wished Sloane would realize they were perfect for each other too. Would she bring the new boyfriend with her? Max couldn't stop the anger and betrayal he felt thinking of Sloane with another man. What would happen if he saw them together? If anyone knew about this new guy it would be Foster. Bella would have told him something.

"How's Sloane been? There haven't been any sightings of any of Petrov's family around, has there?"

"She's doing okay. We haven't seen much of her since she moved, but Bella and her don't go a day without talking."

"Too busy with the new boyfriend, I guess."

"What boyfriend?"

"Sloane told me she was seeing someone the last time I saw her."

"That's news to me, man."

"Really? I figured Bella would have at least mentioned someone."

"That's just it, she would have, and I didn't hear anything."

"Huh."

"She's had around-the-clock surveillance since she moved. She doesn't know it, but Mother, Tank, and Gutter Mouth have all pitched in to keep an eye on her. We installed a security system in her apartment too."

"You should have told me. I could have helped ease the load."

"I wanted to, man. Bella made it very clear to me I wasn't to tell you anything to lead you to her door."

"I can't blame her. I tried to make her talk to me. Explain it was a misunderstanding, only she wouldn't let me. Claimed she had moved on already. Maybe the guys would know about her mystery man?"

"Maybe, although no one mentioned it to me. I gave instructions to background anyone who comes and goes from that building. Just to be safe."

Could she have gone back to Brody and just didn't want to get the third degree from Mirabella and Foster? No, there's no way she would have gone back to him. Plus, the guys would have ratted her out for that in a heartbeat. The men piled into Ren's car. Ren drove with Bella's father, Clint, in

166

the passenger seat. Max and Foster sat together in the back.

They pulled up to the small church, parking in the side lot. Max followed the rest of the guys inside. He entered the narthex, immediately inhaling the familiar scent of burning incense. The pews before him were adorned with white lilies, as was the altar. Turning to find Foster and the other men, Max bumped into a tall older man with a shaved head. Colorful tattoos peaked out of his button-down shirt at the wrists and neck.

"I'm sorry, sir. I wasn't watching where I was going."

"No worries, son. I was looking for Clint; any idea where I could find him?"

"Yes, sir. I'm going that way myself, if you'd like to follow me."

"Ah, you must be the best man, Maxwell. We've heard a lot about you."

"That would be me. And you are?"

"I'm Logan."

Max shook the man's offered hand. They walked together down the hall into the tower room being used to corral the men until the ceremony. He knew if he walked the opposite direction, he'd find Sloane in the other tower room. He missed her. Not a day went by that he didn't think about her. Although more and more these days he wondered: Who was the lucky bastard that got to see that smile that made his heart soar? Steeling himself, he decided it didn't matter who this other guy was. Somehow he would fix this.

Logan knocked on the closed door with authority

and opened it without waiting for a response. The other men were joking and hugging him before Max closed the door.

"'Bout time you got here," Clint teased.

"You know what it was like getting Marigold and Poppy out of the house?" Logan said.

Ren let out a belly laugh. "I do not envy you, buddy!"

"It was *not* a good time, that's for damn sure," Logan replied.

Foster smiled at the man. "Good to see you again, Mr. Robertson. I see you've met Max."

"I did, and I told you last time, it's Logan."

"Mr. Robertson?" Max took a moment to study the man more closely. He looked to be close to six-foot-one, and his bald head and tattoos would make him intimidating to most people. He now knew where Sloane got her eyes. "Sloane's father?"

"The one and only."

A knock sounded on the door as it was opening. A small man with a full head of dark hair entered the room. The roman collar gave away that he was their priest.

"It's time to take your places, gentlemen."

Clint stopped before the large doors that led into the nave to wait for his daughter. Max followed Foster toward the altar to take his place next to him as his best man. Logan and Ren took their seats.

"I'm really happy for you, man."

"Thanks, Max. I couldn't have found a better woman."

"True, Bella is special."

"Sloane is too."

Max nodded his head once stiffly. Foster was getting his happily ever after. Why the hell couldn't Max? The rest of the guests were seated quickly. It was a small ceremony. Just family and close friends would be attending. Unfortunately, that meant partners too. Max watched Brody walk down the aisle and take a seat. The woman he had on his arm was the same stripper from the club. She looked like she was working the corner after the ceremony, in a red mini dress two sizes too small.

"Why the hell would he bring her?"

"They've been seeing each other publicly ever since Sloane ended it," Foster whispered back.

"How do you think she's going to react?"

"I guess we'll see."

As if on cue, the music changed dramatically. All the guests stood up, facing the back of the church. The doors once again opened. Slowly and confidently, Sloane began her walk down the aisle. Max felt his knees weaken. His heart beat rapidly in his chest. She was absolutely breathtaking. The black of the dress gave her pale skin an angelic glow. There were no sleeves, and her bare arms brought to mind a vision of her in his bed with the sheets barely covering her. Max had to stifle that train of thought. He couldn't afford to sport a hard-on in church.

Her golden hair was pulled back off of her face. For the first time she didn't need to push her bangs from her face. Her eyes locked on him as she continued toward the altar. Max wanted to rush down to her and take her into his arms, but he restrained himself. This was Foster and Bella's day.

Sloane took her place on the opposite side of the aisle. Again, the music shifted.

***

Sloane

Sloane could feel everyone's eyes on her. It was kinda creepy, actually. Perhaps she should just elope when she got married. She laughed to herself. She'd need a boyfriend first. Fat chance of that, seeing as soon she'd have a baby bump.

She glanced over at Foster. He had his signature smirk on his face. Probably thinking of ways to tease her about how put together she was. For once.

As much as she tried not to look at Max, she couldn't help herself. Damn, he looked good. Too good. She couldn't take her traitorous eyes off of him. Miraculously, she made it to the front of the room without falling on her face. She'd count that as a win.

As the music changed, everyone faced the back again to see the bride, everyone except Sloane. She watched Foster. The look of pure adoration that crossed his face made her heart swell. One look at his expression and you could never doubt his feelings for her.

"Who gives this woman to this man?"

"I do," Sloane's Uncle Clint answered.

He lifted Bella's veil before placing a kiss on her cheek. Then he took his seat next to Aunt Marigold and Sloane's parents. As Father McMurphy began his sermon, Sloane let her mind wander. What would it be like to be loved the way Bella was loved by Foster? As she stood there feeling out of place in her gown, she could feel Max's eyes. Taking her gaze off the happy couple, she looked into the eyes of the man she loved. His expression was guarded. His eyes however, never left hers. It wasn't until the congregation was alive with applause, did she realize Mr. and Mrs. Hyland were sharing their first kiss as husband and wife.

Sloane clapped along with everyone else. When Bella turned to walk out with her new husband, Sloane fixed her train before taking her place next to Max. She threaded her hand through his arm. Her stupid heart kicked up its tempo to double time as Max placed his other hand over hers. The man simply didn't know what one touch, however insignificant, could do to her. She kept her eyes straight ahead and tried like hell to concentrate on putting one high-heeled foot in front of the other.

"You look beautiful," he said. Sloane hoped Max couldn't hear her breath hitch.

"Thank you," she whispered.

They took their places beside Bella and Foster in the receiving line. Their job was to thank the guests for coming and remind them of the reception being held out back in the gardens.

"Sloane…" a familiar, and unwanted, voice said.

"Hello, Brody." She smiled, still standing there with Max.

"You look gorgeous."

"Ahem." The trashy looking woman next to Brody coughed loudly.

Instead of introducing her, Brody grabbed a hold

of her arm roughly, directing her outside. That went better than expected. It's funny. Sloane always thought she would want to claw the other woman's eyes out if she ever saw her, but she didn't. Oddly enough, she felt nothing but relief. He was her problem now. Sloane held her head up a little higher after that. It was a good feeling.

The gardens were decorated to look like something out of a fairytale. The sun was just beginning to set on the horizon. Reds, oranges, and yellows painted the sky. One by one each tree lit up with hundreds of little lights. Larger paper lanterns hung from wires above the tables and stone dance floor. It was magical. Every detail was exactly how Bella had envisioned it.

Sloane walked arm in arm with Max to the head table where they both took their seats—Max to the left of Foster and Sloane to the right of Bella. At least she wouldn't feel she had to make conversation with him all night.

Someone in the crowd started to tap their glass with a spoon, inciting giggles and catcalls from the crowd gathered. Bella beamed up at Foster as he leaned down to kiss her tenderly. As the laughter and noise died down, Sloane slid back in her chair and stood up.

"Thank you all for being here tonight to celebrate the union of two of the best people I've had the privilege to know. Growing up, Bella was like the big sister I never had…and didn't want." The crowd laughed as Sloane continued. "We did virtually everything together. She was and always will be my best friend."

She turned to smile at the couple. "I've watched the both of you together for some time now. I truly believe you are made for each other. No one completes Bella the way you do, Foster. I see it every day in the way you love each other. I wish you a long and blessed life together."

Sloane raised the sparkling cider that she'd switched out, as everyone else toasted with champagne. She sat back down as Max stood up.

"I'm not a big fan of speeches, so I'll keep mine short and sweet. Over the years I've known Foster, I have never seen him look at a woman the way he looks at you, Bella. You are his world. If he were asked to describe his perfect woman, I have no doubts he would describe you to a T. It's truly humbling to see two people so much in love. No one completes Foster the way you do, Bella. I wish you both all the happiness in the world."

Max sat down and glasses clinked all over the garden once again. The meal was brought out and Sloane ate it as if someone was going to steal it from her. She didn't realize how hungry she was until that first bite.

"Damn, did you taste any of it?" Bella laughed as she whispered in her ear.

"You know; I don't think I did." She joined in with her own laughter.

"I would now like to call Mr. and Mrs. Hyland to the floor for their first dance as husband and wife," the reception assistant announced.

Foster stood up, holding out his hand to Bella. He led her to the center of the dance floor. The melody for a familiar song started to play. Sloane was overjoyed watching Bella's dreams come true. Once the DJ began playing for the crowd to dance, Sloane made her way over to her parents.

"There's my beautiful baby girl." Her father squeezed her in one of his bear hugs.

"Looking pretty handsome yourself tonight, Daddy."

Sloane stretched up on tiptoes to kiss her father's cheek. He was a big man with tattoos and muscles to spare. His contagious laugh was one of her favorite sounds. To see his six-foot-one frame next to her mother's five-foot-three always made her giggle. Especially because she knew who was in charge of that relationship, and it wasn't the man that intimidated all her boyfriends when she was a teenage girl.

"Seems a certain gentleman can't keep his eyes off of you. Do I need to put him in his place?"

Excitement flooded through her as she turned to look in the same direction as her father did. Only it wasn't Max like she'd hoped. Sloane's heart felt like it dropped into her stomach. Kasper smiled, saluting her with his drink. She smiled and waved back.

"He's harmless, Daddy. Just a good friend. One of the men who was trying to help me."

"Have they found that man yet?" Concern etched into her father's face.

"Not yet, but I can't continue to live my life in constant fear. I trust in them. They'll find him."

"My brave girl. How about a dance with your old man?"

"I'd love to."

Sloane let her father lead her out onto the floor. She never had to be afraid of anything when she was with him. The little girl in her knew without a doubt nothing could harm her when he was near. The smile she had been wearing was lost however, as her eyes landed on Max across the room. A petite brunette was giggling as she ran her hand up and down his arm. He smiled that sexy mischievous grin that always made Sloane melt inside. Only she didn't melt this time because it wasn't directed at her.

"What's wrong, baby girl?"

"Nothing."

"That sad look in your eye isn't nothing to me."

"Just a boy, Daddy."

"Would that boy be Max?"

"How do you know Max?"

"A father always knows about the important things, and people, in his baby girl's life. Are you in love with him?"

"Yes. I was, I still am."

"Well, if he's passin' up you for that girl, he's an idiot and I don't think I want you with someone that stupid."

"Daddy!" She laughed, but her heart wasn't really in it.

Max swiped a loose hair from the girl's cheek. Just like he did with her. Sloane watched the woman swoon—actually *swoon*. This was excruciating. Sloane wondered if anyone else could tell that she was dying inside. He was killing her. He couldn't wait until she wasn't around? Then again, for Max, it was probably just another

Saturday night.

Not for her. This was just another reminder of why she was here alone. Max was looking for his next warm body. Not someone to share his life with. Sloane needed a man who wanted to be there for all the mundane day-to-day tasks. She needed a man willing to be a father. Not a playboy. Her hand went to her stomach.

"I think I need a few moments alone."

"Are you sure you're going to be all right?"

"Of course I will be." She paused before adding, "In time."

Sloane kissed her father's cheek before weaving through the bodies on the crowded dance floor. She headed back toward the church. She'd spotted a bench on the way out to the garden after the ceremony. She thought it would be a good place to gather herself before she had to fake a smile in front of everyone again. She sat there listening to the sound of Luke Bryan coming from the DJ's speakers.

"Hey there, Darlin'."

Kasper smiled down at her. He looked damn good in his three-piece suit. The blue of his shirt made his eyes sparkle. His smile lit up his whole face. No, Kasper didn't look good, he looked hot as hell. Unfortunately, he didn't make her heart race the way Max did. She wished like hell he would.

"Where's your date, Cowboy?"

"I didn't bring one. Didn't see you here with anyone either. Coincidence?" He waggled his eyebrows. Sloane couldn't help but laugh. Kasper always did that, at least. He was an invaluable friend in that capacity. Over the past few weeks he would call or text her, saying things just to get a laugh out of her. She appreciated that more than he could ever know.

"I'm not interested in men right now."

"Is this about a certain someone we both know, that can act like a douche from time to time? Or should I get a video camera, a date, and meet you back at your place?" He grinned.

She didn't know if she should confess to him or brush it off as nothing. They were friends, after all. He lifted her chin with his fingertips, and she felt the tears well up in her eyes. She rapidly blinked them back. The concern on Kasper's face made her decision for her.

"Yes," she whispered.

"You love him?"

"More than I thought I could."

"Then why are you sitting out here by yourself? Go to him."

"It's too late. See for yourself." She nodded back toward the celebration.

***

Max

Max downed another shot of whiskey before pulling Sara—no, Tara—out to the edge of the dance area. He pressed their bodies together, swaying to the music. She practically purred in his ear. He pictured Sloane in his arms instead. He ran his hands over her curves as they moved. The girl in his arms was all wrong for the girl he pictured in his head. Sloane was soft and smooth. Her skin felt like expensive silk. This imposter couldn't hold a candle to her no matter how much he wished she could.

He opened his eyes, his gaze drifting over to a wooden bench under a tree. Staring back at him, Gutter Mouth slowly shook his head. What the fuck was his problem? As his old friend stood up, Max could see Sloane sitting there. Shit. Had they both been watching him dance with Kara or was it Sara? Not like her name mattered. It wasn't Sloane. He released the woman in his arms mid-song. She looked up at him, confused.

"I'm sorry, I have to go."

"I can come with you."

She ran her hand down his arm, giving a seductive little smile, but it was wasted on him. He wasn't interested in her or any other woman here. Without answering, Max marched off to find Sloane and Gutter Mouth. The bench they sat at before was empty now. He scanned the area until he spotted them up ahead, walking toward the front of the church holding hands. Jealousy reared its ugly head again.

"Sloane," he yelled to get her attention. Either she didn't hear him or she was ignoring him. He yelled again. This time she stopped walking. Her hand still in Gutter Mouth's, she looked over her shoulder at him. Max quickly closed the distance between them.

"We need to talk. Now."

"I don't think we do, Max."

"Darlin'—"

"Kasper, I adore you, but you need to shut up."

Gutter Mouth held up his hands in surrender. Max watched them exchange a look. There was an unknown agreement in that look.

"Is this who you're seeing? Is that why you haven't told anyone?" he demanded.

"No, Max. I'm not seeing Kasper. We're friends."

"Then why won't—"

A light twinkled from the trees nearby just before Gutter Mouth shoved Sloane toward Max and reached for the gun at his waist. Shots rang out, and Max launched himself at her, knocking them both to the ground. A sharp pain stabbed him as he rolled them so her body wouldn't be the point of impact. Her screams echoed in his head as Max pulled his revolver from his ankle holster, firing in the same direction as Gutter Mouth was. Max knew he had to protect Sloane at all costs.

Max couldn't tell whose bullet hit Booker in the side of his face, but it didn't matter who pulled the trigger. All that mattered was that the man was down and couldn't fire another round at Sloane. Lifting his body from hers, Max assessed her for wounds.

"Where are you hit?"

"I-I'm not. At least I don't think so."

"There's blood on you, baby. Let me look. Hold still."

Sloane lay there with her arms to her sides as Max's hands roamed over her. He was looking for the bullet hole, but he couldn't deny it felt good to touch her again, even if the circumstances sucked.

179

There was blood on her hands and dress, only he couldn't find a wound anywhere. Max stood up to help Sloane to her feet only to sway on his own. His vision began to blur as he dropped down to his knees.

"Max? Are you okay?"

"I'm fine. Just a little dizzy."

Sloane began pushing and pulling on his clothes. It would've been a turn-on if she didn't look scared to death. Shouts were coming from the garden as guests began running out toward all the commotion. The color drained from her face.

"Kasper! He's been hit!" Sloane called, wide eyed.

Kasper knelt down next to him and lifted up the left side of his shirt. Max looked down. There was a small hole in his side closer to his back. Kasper ripped Max's shirt open and removed it, balling it up into a thick wad. Max could feel the wound pull as the fabric was ripped off.

"Sloane, listen to me," Gutter Mouth said. "Press this on the wound tightly and don't take it off."

"He's gonna be okay, right? Damn you, Max. You better be okay!"

"I'll be fine, baby."

Max looked into her beautiful eyes. They glistened as tears rolled down her cheeks. He could hear Foster talking to Gutter Mouth. He had no idea if he would really be fine, but he couldn't stand to see her hurting. He would promise anything to erase that pained look from her beautiful face. He could hear sirens in the distance. If he could just keep his eyes open long enough for them to arrive. Max felt some of the pain subside as his side began to go numb.

The paramedics came rushing over. They moved Sloane aside, barking orders at everyone hovering. Max felt the pull once again as the medic removed the shirt from the wound. The men talked above him asking him questions. His head felt fuzzy. He supposed it was okay for him to close his eyes now.

Chapter Sixteen

Sloane

"Sloane! Oh my God! What the hell happened?"

Mirabella ran toward her, wrapping Sloane in her arms. Sloane squeezed her back, but only for a moment. All she wanted was to be with Max. She needed to be with him. She ran toward the ambulance, jumping in the back before the man could close the door all the way.

"I'm coming."

"Only family, ma'am."

"He's my fiancé," she blurted. Shit, it worked for him last time. Why not her?

"Okay, but sit back and stay out of the way."

"Yes, sir."

The man's name badge read Murphy. Sloane couldn't figure out if it was his first name or his last. Paramedic Murphy continued hooking Max up to numerous machines. Calling out things about his pulse ox, blood pressure, and other vitals that she had no clue as to what they actually measured. It was surreal. She couldn't believe Max had been shot. He'd taken a bullet. For her. It was hard for her to breathe. She'd always known he would protect her from harm, but she'd never really thought about how. She certainly never thought it would lead to him being shot.

Sloane felt the first tear fall before she could stop it. Taking Max's hand gently, she leaned forward and whispered in his ear.

"Don't leave me, Max. I can't do this without you."

His eyes fluttered opened slowly. She leaned over him, ready to tell him he had to be okay. He just had to, because he was going to be a father. However, before she could get the words out, Murphy moved her away.

"Sir, can you tell me your name?"

"Max."

"Can you tell me what happened?"

"Sloane?"

"Your fiancée is fine. What happened to you?"

"Shot."

Max began coughing in between responses. Panic bubbled up inside of Sloane. Red foam began seeping from his lips. The paramedic continued to write things on his clipboard. When they reached the hospital, the back doors opened as more men and women in scrubs pulled out the gurney that held Max. She followed them inside and down the hall until a nurse stopped her just as they wheeled him into surgery.

"Miss, you need to stay here. The doctors will do everything they can."

Then she was gone. Sloane don't know how or when she made her way to the waiting room, but that's where she was when the doctor found her. She looked up at him.

"Maxwell Fear's family?"

"Yes, Doctor. How is he?"

Sloane held her breath as strong arms wrapped around her from behind. Startled, she turned to find it was Kasper holding her. Foster and Bella were also standing there along with others that Sloane didn't know, but recognized from the wedding. Foster was holding an elderly woman in his arms.

"When did you guys get here?"

"Oh honey, about an hour ago. You were so out of it; you didn't respond to any of us." Bella hugged her.

Sloane turned back to the doctor in disbelief.

"Maxwell suffered from a gunshot wound to the lateral thoracic. It caused a significant amount of blood loss and collapsed a lung. We've stopped the bleeding and re-inflated his lung."

"Oh my God. Is he going to be okay?"

"I believe he'll make a full recovery. He's out of surgery now. Once he's in a private room, I'll send a nurse to get you."

The doctor patted her shoulder before turning and walking down the hallway. Sloane plopped herself down in the nearest chair. Bella took the one next to her. Sloane put her head on her cousin's shoulder. She felt the tears start all over again.

"It's okay, honey. He's gonna be just fine. You heard the doctor."

"I could have lost him, Bella. I could have lost

184

him today and he never would have known. I never told him."

"Oh, don't think such things. Deep down I'm sure he knows you love him. We all do." She smiled down at her.

"Not that. Bella...I'm pregnant," Sloane whispered.

"What?" the elderly woman called from halfway across the waiting room. She must've had her hearing aids on full freakin' blast to have heard Sloane. She felt like a big spotlight was shining on her now. "What did you just say?"

"I...um...I'm sorry, who are you?" she stammered as the elderly woman removed herself from Foster's arms. She made her way over to where Sloane sat with Bella. Moving slowly, but gracefully, the woman stopped in front of her. Sloane stood up because it felt wrong to be seated.

"I'm Adeline. Max's grandmother."

"Oh my..."

"Oh my, is one way to put it."

"Addy, what's going on?"

A middle-aged woman approached them. She had short auburn hair that framed a round face with gentle eyes. She was beautiful. Only the slightest smudge of her eye makeup indicated her worry for Max. Max's grandmother took the woman's hands in her own. A smile turned her lip up slightly.

"I believe this is the young lady Max has been telling you about."

The woman's attention shifted back to her. "You're Sloane?"

"Yes, ma'am. I am."

"I'm Caroline. Max's mother. It's nice to finally meet you." Her smile was so genuine that Sloane was slightly taken aback. Max never spoke about his family before. She wasn't sure he had one. She had no idea why he would talk about her to them.

"I'm so sorry. This is all my fault."

"Don't. This is what my Max does. He protects people for a living. Every job runs a risk. We all know that."

A job. It all boils down to that. Sloane felt stupid that she had almost forgotten. It made sense now. Of course Max told his family about his work. Sloane talked about work with her family. Now that job was done and Max would move on again. Caroline wiped a single tear from her cheek. Sloane straightened her shoulders. She would tell Max about the pregnancy because he deserved to know, but she would be clear in telling him he had no obligations.

"Now dear, what was it that you were saying?"

"I'm sorry, what?" Sloane feigned ignorance, but his grandmother was a smart cookie.

"Nice try. How far along are you?"

Caroline's eyes widened. "Oh my."

"My thoughts exactly." Sloane tried to smile. "I'm about two months along."

Adeline nodded. "Well, this changes everything."

"I don't see how."

"He doesn't know."

It wasn't a question. Adeline was simply making a statement. The door leading to the lobby opened. A weight pressed against Sloane's chest as Charlie scanned the small waiting room. She had her hair pulled back with rose-colored scrubs on. Spotting Foster, she hurried over to him.

"How is he, Foster?"

"The doctor said he would be fine."

She gasped, pressing a hand to her chest. "Thank God."

"How did you know he was here?"

"I was bringing a patient to surgery. I noticed his name on the board."

Charlie looked up, and their eyes met across the room. The hate and anger radiating off of the woman could practically be seen, it was so thick. Foster grabbed her arm, but she shook him off with a dirty look and a jerk of her arm. Pointing a perfectly manicured finger at Sloane, she closed the distance.

"You. This is all your fault, you bitch," she screamed.

"Excuse me, who are you?" Adeline crossed her arms over her chest.

"Charlie, this isn't the time," Foster warned her.

"I've been seeing Max for a while now. I guess you could call me his girlfriend."

"Charlie, don't—" Foster's plea went unnoticed.

"Really? Max never mentioned you to us. He always tells us the important parts of his life. *Especially* women."

"We've been seeing each other for almost a year." Charlie sounded surprised.

"And yet, we've never even heard him speak your name before. What does that tell you?"

Tears ran down Charlie's face. Her mouth hung

slightly agape. Sloane would've felt bad, if she wasn't such a bitch to her. Sloane watched her face harden. Charlie glared at her.

"Don't think for one minute that he won't drop you just as quickly when the next pretty face comes along."

"I'm not your competition, Charlie. I know better than to try and tie him down. That's why I called it off with Max weeks ago."

Caroline placed her hand on Sloane's shoulder, urging Sloane to turn and look at her. "That's why you ended it?"

"Yes, ma'am. I need stability in my…situation. I'm not built for a two a.m. phone call when he's lonely."

"Go to Hell," Charlie spat.

"I'm not judging you. If you're okay with that kind of relationship, good for you. I just know I'm not."

Charlie eyed her angrily. "I'm a stronger woman than you, that's why. He'll be back. He *always* comes back."

Adeline waved her pointed finger around. "Well that's horse wash. Sloane is willing to walk away from the man she loves because she won't settle for less than she deserves. That's what I call strength."

Caroline smiled. "Well said, Addy."

"You make me sound like a martyr." Sloane couldn't help but laugh. "In reality, I'm just selfish. I want it all or nothing."

A short round nurse interrupted.

"Max is awake now and asking for a Sloane."

"Go on, dear. Tell him." Adeline patted her

shoulder.

"Yes, ma'am."

Taking a deep breath, Sloane followed the nurse to Max's room. The woman opened the door for her before ushering her inside. Max lay there with his eyes closed, his chest rising and falling with each breath. Beeping machines were the only sound in the room. He should have looked fragile lying there like he was, but she could never see Max as anything other the epitome of strength.

Approaching the side of the bed, she placed her hand on his. Max opened his eyes slowly. His radiant smile almost melted her right there and then. What she wouldn't give to be on the receiving end of it every day.

"You're here."

"Thank you so much."

"I told you I would keep you safe."

"Yes, you did."

Max groaned. He probably couldn't feel much from all the painkillers, but he looked exhausted. "We…need to have a conversation."

"I agree." She sighed.

"Good."

***

Max

Max knew Sloane felt guilty about him getting shot. It was wrong to exploit that, but he would worry about that later. Right now he had to tell her how he felt and make her stay. He patted the space on the bed beside him. Sloane slowly lowered herself onto the mattress.

"I know we don't know everything about each other. I've never really wanted to know much more than what gets a woman off, to be honest with you. I've seen too many relationships go south to actually want to be in one."

"I know, Max. I'm not asking you for one."

"Let me finish. I never believed my Gram when she told me one day I'd find a woman who would make me want to spend every moment with her. I do now. I've missed you, Sloane. I've missed your smile, your laugh, the way you look at me. I want to be with you. I see everything I never knew I wanted in a woman when I look at you."

Sloane was crying. Was that a good thing or a bad thing? Her blue eyes shimmered. Max hoped like hell that they were tears of joy. She lowered her head to try to hide it from him, but it was too late. He couldn't lose her. He pressed on.

"I'm ruined, baby. No one else will do. You're all I want. You're everything I need and I refuse to let you walk away again without a fight. Do you understand that? Look at me, Sloane."

She raised her head. She was still in her gown with his blood covering part of her dress and arm. Most of her hair was still pulled back except those damn bangs had come loose. Max pushed them off of her face. He used the motion to allow him to cup her cheek. He stroked his thumb across the smooth skin a few times. She leaned into his touch. She was so damn beautiful. With a pounding heart, Max decided it was time to go all in.

"I refuse to let you go. I love you, Sloane."

"You what?" She gasped.

"I love you, baby."

Sloane stood up and paced the room. Now he was starting to worry. He thought for sure she was going to turn and walk out. He didn't know what else he could say to make her stay, but he needed to come up with something.

"You love me?" She whispered it like a prayer.

"Absofuckinlutely."

"Max..."

She took her bottom lip in between her teeth, worrying it as she sat down beside him again. She looked unsure of herself. He knew the moment she gained the courage she was looking for. Her shoulders squared and she sat up straighter, determination painting her face.

"There's no easy way to say this to you, so I'm just going to say it. You're going to be a father."

Of all the things he thought she would say to him, that wasn't one of them. Not even close. He was going to be a father. He understood the words. He just couldn't reconcile them pertaining to him.

"You're pregnant."

"Yes, Max, I'm pregnant."

Max felt the smile spreading across his face. He was going to be a father. His baby was growing in her belly. Pride swelled inside him. He tried to sit up, but the pain forced him to lie back down. Instead he held his arm open for her.

"Are you okay? Did you pull your stitches?"

"I don't care, Sloane. I just want you in my arms. Come here."

"Max no, you're hurt."

"Now." The firmness in his voice left no room to argue.

Sloane carefully climbed into the small hospital bed with him. She put her head on his shoulder and her hand over his heart. He was in pain and beyond tired, but he had the woman he loved in his arms and his future growing inside of her. Nothing could top this moment of pure happiness.

"Max," she whispered against his shoulder.

"Yeah, baby?"

She looked up at him, meeting his eyes. Tears still glistened in hers. Her smile lit up every dark spot in his soul.

"I love you too, Max."

Her soft kiss was like a promise. A promise of their future together. Just like that, Sloane topped his best moment ever. He knew without a doubt she would continue to do so for years to come and he couldn't wait.

Epilogue

Max

Max watched as Mia struggled to keep herself from falling back down on her cute little diapered butt. At ten months old, she was already growing up too quickly for his liking. These were his favorite moments. Sitting out in the yard while his daughter played on the blanket beside him. The wonder in her eyes as she took in her surroundings was a salve to his soul. All of the shitty things he saw as a cop and then as a PI had begun to jade him. Mia helped restore his faith in humanity.

He'd never expected to trust a woman enough to fall in love. Finding Sloane had changed him in the best possible way. She made him want to be a better man. He couldn't be more grateful to be able to call her his own. Her sweet voice broke him from his thoughts.

"I thought we agreed that she could wait on a puppy, Max?"

"We did, but look at her, baby. She's already in

love."

Sloane sat next to Max on the blanket. Their daughter giggled loudly as she played with the cutest ball of yellow fur. The eight-week-old golden retriever was a perfect addition to their little family. Yes, Max had agreed to wait until Mia was a toddler before buying a dog, but one look at the pup and Max couldn't pass him up.

"What can I say? When you're right, you're right. He's absolutely adorable."

"Can I get that in writing?" He laughed.

"That he's adorable? Sure."

"No, that I'm right?"

"No, you may not."

Sloane smiled sweetly at him, leaning over to steal a kiss. Almost two years later and her kisses still ignited the fire within him. He lifted her hand up and kissed the back of it. Her diamond engagement ring sparkled in the sunlight.

"When are you going to set a date and make an honest man outta me?"

"When we aren't so busy that I can take the time to drop what's left of this weight."

"There's nothing for you to drop. You're even more beautiful than when we first met."

Sure, her belly wasn't as taunt as before, and there were stretch marks where there was once smooth skin, but Max didn't care about those things. Sloane was gorgeous. The fact that she had given him a healthy, happy, beautiful baby girl only made him want her more.

"Max." She scowled, rolling her eyes at him.

"I'm serious. Everything around here will be

relatively settled in a few weeks. Don't keep me waiting."

"I can't plan a wedding in a few weeks, Max." She laughed at his eagerness.

"Okay, okay. Soon, though?"

"Soon, Max, soon."

Sloane moved herself between his legs. He opened them into a V shape to allow her to sit. She pressed her back to his chest, and Max wrapped his arms around her. They watched Mia play with her new friend.

"So what time will the guys be over in the morning? Do you want me to make breakfast?"

For now, Max was conducting business out of his small home office until the building he leased was ready to move in. He was waiting for the landlord to give him the green light. As of last month all the proper licensing had come in. His dream of being his own boss was finally a reality. Once he knew it was going to happen, he called Tank, Mother, and Gutter Mouth. They all agreed to take on a role in the company. Max couldn't be happier. He had it all: an amazing, soon-to-be wife, a sweet baby girl, and a bright future, heading up his own company.

"No way, you're *my* woman. If you don't stop feeding them, they'll never go out and find their own," he teased.

"Yes, dear. Can you answer one thing for me?"

"Anything."

"Why in God's name would you name that sweet little puppy, 'Killer'?"

"Why not?" he asked innocently as she erupted

with laughter.

"I love you, Maxwell Fear. I don't know what I'm going to do with you, but I sure as hell love you."

"I love you, baby. I can think of a few things you can do with me." He waggled his eyebrows at her. His cell phone chimed from his pocket. "Hold that thought."

He swiped his finger across the screen to answer. Sloane watched him expectantly as he said, "thank you" and disconnected. He smiled down at her before kissing her soft lips.

"Fear Incorporated is officially open for business."

The End.

Acknowledgments

Thank you to everyone who had a hand in making this project the best it could be: Lori, Sydnee, Dimitri, Jennifer, and everyone else behind the scenes at Limitless Publishing. You guys rock.

To my fellow Limitless authors, thank you for all of your support. Your shares, likes, and wisdom have been invaluable. I'm honored to be a part of the Limitless family.

To my family. Thank you for understanding things like deadlines and late nights and that yes, a grown woman can and will pout because a scene isn't working. Thank you for understanding my coffee addiction and providing me the necessary amount of Raisinets to help me keep my sanity. I love you.

Finally, to my readers, thank you from the bottom of my heart for letting me share my stories with you. I hope you're looking forward to reading more about the Men of Fear Incorporated as much as I am to write them. Much love, Melinda.

About the Author

Melinda Valentine was born in upstate New York. Being the youngest of four children (and the only girl) made it easy for her to turn to books as companions. As a young child, she was whisked away to Baltimore, Maryland and spent her youth reading books such as *Nancy Drew*, *The Chronicles of Narnia,* and *The Little House on the Prairie* saga.

However, it wasn't until she was twelve years old that she read a book (Stephen King's *IT*) that made her realize that someday, she would herself become a writer. After that, her first (horrible) manuscript came to life, and at thirteen she had received her very first rejection letter. Heartbroken, she continued to read even more to learn about the craft of writing.

Today Melinda calls West Virginia home, with her husband and their three hilarious children. She works full time as a bank teller and creates characters she hopes her readers fall in love with as much as she has.

Facebook:
https://www.facebook.com/authormelindavalentine

Twitter:
https://twitter.com/author_melindav

Website:
http://www.melindavalentine.com/

Made in the USA
Middletown, DE
23 June 2016